LOCO

He didn't know his parents and he had no friends. He didn't even have a proper name. The name he went by was Loco—and he'd won that handle in a hundred wild shoot-outs on both sides of the Rio Grande.

Loco never had to look for trouble, he just naturally drifted into it. But this time it seemed to come out of the clear blue when a bullet dropped his horse from under him. He looked up into the barrel of a stranger's gun—and heard the click of the hammer being cocked.

Loco should have been scared. But being Loco, he just started to get mad . . .

LOCO

Lee Hoffman

GUNSMOKE

First published in the UK by Tandem Books

This hardback edition 2008
by BBC Audiobooks Ltd
by arrangement with
Golden West Literary Agency

ISBN 978 1 405 68192 6

British Library Cataloguing in Publication Data available.

Printed and bound in Great Britain by
Antony Rowe Ltd., Chippenham, Wiltshire

CHAPTER 1

The tobiana mare might be a little long in the tooth, but she had a smooth, easy single-foot that she could hold all day. The man in the saddle was thankful for that. All in all, he figured, she wasn't a bad horse. Sure as good as a man could hope for when he had to steal the first mount he could get his hands on.

He did wish he'd had time to shop around for a saddle though. The misfitting old Mexican *silla* was meant to be cushioned with a *mochila,* not ridden with his rump against the crude rawhide-covered tree.

The long ride had been tiring, especially those first days. He'd been pushing hard, anxious to get north of the Rio Bravo, and then to put distance between it and himself. He rode easier now. They sure wouldn't cross the river after him—would they?

And it looked like he'd be reaching his destination soon. He rode the slopes of a jagged range crusted with aspen and fir. The bald gray face on the peak rising to his left looked like the landmark that Ray deVaca had described to him. He wondered if Ray had made it across the river.

There were still patches of snow on some of the slopes. Runoff from them flooded small streams. Bright spring green poked out of the ground and speckled the branches of bushes. It gave the crisp breeze spicy scents. Chokecherries waved fresh white blossoms at him. The aspen twinkled in the bright sun, under a sky as clean and clear and wide-open with promise as tomorrow. It was good country, he thought. And a good day. A day for appreciating the fact that his blood was still running warm through his veins instead of staining some bare parched clay back yonder, across the river.

The aspen leaves put him in mind of silver dollars. What would it be like if they were, and a man could pluck all the coin he needed off the trees? Would everybody have a full belly and a warm bed then? He wished his own belly were full. Felt hungrier than a toothless hound. Even so, he whistled cheerfully as he rode. It was a good day.

He'd been easing his saddle-stiff legs, riding with the right one hooked around the gourd horn and the other loose of the awkward carved-wood stirrup. When he spotted a trail cutting down the slope, he swung astride again. It was a mistake.

Finding the stirrups, he leaned out of the saddle for a better look at the ground. The moist dark earth showed sharp prints of iron-shod hoofs. With a satisfied nod to himself, he settled and flicked the reins. The mare's rump swayed as she single-footed onto the trail.

He figured with luck he'd be able to chouse up something to eat and a place to bed before nightfall. He sure hoped so. He had cooked the final scant handful of corn-meal for supper last night. There was nothing left but one shriveled hot pepper in his pocket. Plenty of game around, to judge by all the signs, but no way to take it. Hard thing to go hungry in such rich country. Hard thing to go hungry any time, any place.

He was still whistling as he knotted the reins and dropped them over the saddle horn. Lacing his fingers behind his head, he leaned back to flex the weary muscles of his shoulders. Even tired and hungry and anything else, it was still good to be alive.

He felt the lurch almost before he heard the shot.

The mare pitched forward. Instinctively, he kicked the stirrups, trying to jump clear as she fell.

The world wheeled around him. He felt the hard slam of the ground against his right hip and shoulder—an even harder blow against his foot—and he knew he hadn't quite made it. Over nine hundred pounds of limp horse were sprawled across his foot.

He lay face down in the dirt, not stunned, but numb. The bright colors that had flashed inside his head slowly faded. Thoughts broke through them. Had he been wrong? Had they managed to follow him after all? He told himself it wasn't likely. But whatever had happened, he couldn't just lie there thinking about it. He had to do something.

His head didn't want to move. He forced it up. When he got his eyes open, all he could see were wet blurs. He squeezed them shut, then tried opening them again. It was a downright unpleasant sensation. And the numbness he'd felt was changing into a dull, pressing pain. It spread up from his ankle to his knee. As he lifted himself onto his elbows, it reached toward his hip.

He drew a long, deep, weary, disgusted breath and craned his neck to look at the horse. It was a lifeless mound heaped on his right foot. Blood smeared its head. That had been either a helluva good shot or a lucky one— for whoever had fired it. But who? Why?

The wind whispered gently through the trees. A bird made a comment and another answered it. Insects rose from the moist grass to buzz around his face. And his own shallow breathing sounded uncommon loud. There was nothing else to be heard. No rush of horsemen toward him. No crashing or rattling through the bushes. Nothing.

Was it possible that someone hadn't been shooting at him intentionally? Maybe it was just some damn-fool accident. It seemed unlikely, but he'd heard of worse. He wondered if the person who'd fired that shot could have realized his mistake and decided to ignore the results.

Well, whatever had happened, it looked like he was alone with his troubles.

Propped on one elbow, he swatted at the bugs, wiped his face, then looked at the horse again. The bar of the saddle tree seemed to be pressing on his leg above the ankle. Tentatively, he tugged the leg. There was pain, but nothing as sharp as he'd expect from broken bones.

Be thankful for small favors, he told himself. But he'd have felt a lot more thankful for a somewhat larger piece of luck. This shot his plans for the day all to hell and gone. It wasn't going to be easy getting loose.

He got himself leaned back on both elbows, bracing them in the soft earth. With his free foot against the saddle, he pushed and pulled. Nothing happened. Harder. Hell, that hurt. It felt like his leg would come apart at the joints sooner than his foot would slip from under the saddle.

Cursing softly in Spanish, he squirmed toward the horse. The slope of the ground was against him. It took some twisting to get himself sitting up, and he had to lean on his right hand to keep himself that way. Awkward and not exactly comfortable, but it was the only way he could reach in, under the rise of the saddle. He probed his fingers at his boot, the saddle tree, and then the earth. This was going to take work, he decided. Still cursing, he began to scrape at the ground with his fingers.

He sure wished he had something to dig with. Didn't though. Those *Federales* had not only taken his guns and sheath knife, but his boot knife and the hideout knife he'd carried between his shoulder blades. Left him naked but for his clothes.

Well, at least it wasn't hard-baked clay or solid rock he had to excavate. If it had been, he figured he'd likely have a boot full of mush instead of a foot.

He was already tired. Now, in this cramped position, he was really beginning to ache. And his foot hurt. Even the steady string of mumbled profanity didn't help much. What had seemed like a damned fine day had gone to hell in a bucket.

Flinching, he jerked up his head. He peered into the woods with a frown. There'd been a sound of crackling brush. Something moving through the undergrowth. *Not* a lobo, he thought with weary disgust. That was all he needed now, a damned hungry lobo or two.

He couldn't spot whatever was back there in the trees. Listening intently, he answered himself that it was too big and noisy for a wolf. A bear maybe?

No—with a sigh of relief, he realized it must be a horse. And when one lone horse moved at that kind of slow steady walk, it usually had a rider on its back.

He had his mouth open to shout when he thought about that gunshot. Maybe this was the person who'd fired it, finally arriving to see the results. It could be someone who'd tried to kill him—who might still want to do it.

But, hell, if this was a would-be killer searching for him now, there sure wasn't any chance of hiding. He was pinned in place by a lump of horsemeat. He'd be found, no matter what.

And if it wasn't a killer, he sure *wanted* to be found. Taking a deep breath, he gave a holler.

Birds stopped their talk and small things in the grass froze. Even the sound of the horse stopped. He squinted into the shadows, hunting sight of it, and gave another shout.

After a long moment, the sound began again. Then he spotted the horse. It came from the shadows onto the trail above him. He stared in amazement at it and its rider.

The horse was a compact dark bay with the slit ears of an Indian buffalo pony. The rider was a young woman wearing a velvety green riding habit with white lace and a cameo at her throat.

She moved the horse slowly toward him, then halted it.

She sat stiffly in the sidesaddle, with the fabric of her skirt draping down from the knee she had hooked over the horn. It caught on her spur, showing a large sunflower rowel and the high undercut heel of a cowman's boot. The Winchester rifle she held on her knee wasn't just resting there. It was braced. Aimed at him. She gazed at him from under the broad brim of a man's hat with eyes as stony hard and gray as basalt.

It would have been a nice enough face, he thought, if

it'd had a different expression on it. The eyes were deep and wide-set. The nose was a little long but fine-shaped. The mouth was full for kissing. It pinched into a thin, grim line now though. The jaw was strong, maybe a little too square. Hard-knotted muscles at its hinges didn't help. The skin was smooth and lightly tanned. There was an unnatural paleness under the tan though. Brows that should have relaxed in gentle arches drew into a wrinkled frown. Her hair was drawn back and covered by the square-set hat, but if it matched the brows and lashes, it should have been a deep sorrel.

Yeah, it was a real fine face—except that it scowled coldly at him. There was an intensity in the set of it that suggested strong determination. And maybe a touch of fear. He didn't like that at all.

If there was anything he didn't want, it was for someone to point a cocked gun at him and be afraid at the same time. Tight nerves and shaky hands could make a gun hammer drop too easy.

Puzzled by the face he'd never seen before and the rifle that eyed him so unpleasantly, he nodded and smiled. It was the friendliest, most sincere smile he could muster. He knew it was pretty good. It had done just fine for him at other times. Now, though, it got no response.

"I could use some help here," he said hopefully. But from the look of her, she didn't seem very interested in helping.

Gathering her skirt, she slid out of the saddle. It was an easy, graceful move that hardly gave him a glimpse of her boot. Not a sight of bare leg at all. Her hand was wrapped around the action of the rifle, forefinger on the trigger. She let the reins drop, groundhitching the horse, and walked toward him. When she stopped on the far side of the dead mare, she stood as stiffly erect as she'd ridden. Unspeaking, she looked down that fine straight nose at him.

"I got a horse on my foot," he said.

She made no reply.

"I'd be obliged for some help," he tried. But for all the good it did him, he might as well have hollered down a rain barrel. She had nothing resembling concern in her expression. Just cold, hard determination.

Slowly she lifted the muzzle of the gun. She pointed it toward his face.

"Hey! That thing might go off!"

Even as he shouted at her, he had a feeling that was just what she had in mind. *She* was the one who'd shot his horse. He was certain of it.

Staring at the gun, he grunted, *"Dios,* why?"

It was the right question. At least it got an answer. In a voice as icy and grim as the set of her face, she said, "I'm Ruth Caisson."

He took some comfort in the steadiness of her hands on the rifle. With effort, he lifted his eyes to meet hers. "Is that supposed to mean something to me?"

"Three-Slash-C," she offered.

He shook his head. "No, ma'am, never heard of it."

There was a flickering of surprise in her face. "Don't you even know why you're here?"

"No, ma'am. You sure you've got the right man? You *sure* I'm the one you want to shoot?"

"You are the Mexican."

"No, ma'am."

She scanned him, taking in the detail of his snug-legged leather britches with the bone buttons down the sides, the short, braid-trimmed, chaparral jacket held closed by a tied thong, the fancywork at the neck of his grimy *guayabera* shirt, and the rig on the dead horse. It was obvious that she believed his clothes more than she did his words.

"I'm *dressed* Mexican," he told her. "I been in Mexico for a time. But I ain't native to it. You got something against Mexicans?"

She shook her head abstractedly as she studied his face.

He didn't figure his looks would prove anything to her either. He'd passed for Mexican often enough. His face was sharp-boned and sun-darkened, framed with shaggy

LOCO

black hair and set with eyes almost as dark. The lines and
planes of the bones could suggest some Spanish blood, but
they didn't guarantee it.

Just a common ordinary sort of face. There was nothing more special about it than the scar that twisted his
right eyebrow, giving him a perpetual look of bewilderment. A fine face, most of the time. The señoritas liked
it, and nobody else paid much attention to it. Leastways
not usually. Right now, though, the way this girl gazed
at him, he was afraid it wasn't doing him much good at
all. He tried to shape it into bland, smiling innocence.

The girl gestured toward his bone-bare saddle and asked,
"Where's your gun? Your gear?"

"I got none."

She looked doubtful of that, but her grim resolve seemed
to waver. After a moment of thought, she said, "If you're
not the Mexican, who are you?"

"Nobody in particular."

"You've got to have a name."

She sounded so sure of it that he couldn't resist telling
her the truth. "No, ma'am."

"Everybody's got a name."

"I don't."

"That's ridiculous."

"Maybe so, but it's the way things are," he answered,
giving as much of a shrug as he could in the cramped
position he held. As he did it, he tried wiggling his foot.
No good. It was still wedged in too tight to be moved.

Warily she asked him, "What are you doing here?"

"Right this minute, I'm trying to talk you out of shooting me."

She showed some sign of confusion, but she wasn't
amused at all. The small gesture she made with the rifle
was a threat.

"Look, ma'am," he went on hurriedly, "I'm just a mav-
erick. I got no brand, no name, and no owner. I got no
job and no boss. I got no gear, no money, and no gun.
And now it looks like I ain't even got a horse either. You'd

just be wasting your lead and powder shooting me, so why not forget it, huh? Just leave me be, huh?"

She was worse confused now, from the look of her. And she didn't seem nearly so certain that she wanted to kill him. Taking a back step, she let the muzzle of the rifle droop slightly. It was still pointing uncomfortably in his direction, but at least it wasn't staring him in the eye now.

"If you'll excuse me, ma'am," he said, digging his fingers into the ground around his boot again, "I'd sure like to get finished here before sundown."

She stood watching wordlessly as he scraped at the dirt. He could sense her indecision easily enough. She hadn't made up her mind whether she should go ahead and shoot him or not. He wondered if there was any possibility that he *was* the man she wanted to kill.

Keeping his eyes on his work and his voice casual, he said, "If you don't mind me asking, ma'am, just who is it that you want to shoot?"

"That's none of your business."

He glanced sideways at her. "Seems to me as long as you've got that gun pointed at me it kind of *is* some of my business."

She trembled suddenly, quivering like the aspen. For an instant, he thought she was going to break out in tears. The cold composure all disappeared. Color flushed her face and her chin wrinkled. Moisture glistened in her eyes. For that instant, he glimpsed a girl who looked very young and bewildered.

But she fought it. Taking a deep breath, she steadied herself. Her face drew taut again. She said coldly, "Maybe I shouldn't take a chance on you. Maybe I ought to kill you anyway."

She wasn't talking to him, though. He realized she was saying it to herself, auguring herself. He muttered, "I don't think you want to do that."

He could feel a yielding in the pressure on his foot. A few more handfuls of dirt and it might be loose enough. He paused to wipe the sweat filming his face. This time, as he looked toward her, he wasn't smiling. The moment of seeing behind her grim mask still echoed inside him. He added quietly, "I don't think you're really much of a mind to kill anybody."

She didn't meet his eyes. As hard as she tried, she couldn't completely recapture all of that intense determination. She didn't have the sound of ice in her voice as she admitted, "It's not something I *want* to do."

"Then *don't*. Hell, ma'am, killing people is a messy business at best. Sure not anything you want to get mixed up in if you don't have to."

"I have to."

He shook his head. "There must be some other way to handle it. Whatever it is."

"No."

"It ain't nothing the law might give a hand with?"

"No, there isn't any law this side of the ridge. And even if there were, they'd want solid proof. We don't have that." She hesitated, gazing at some distant thought of her own. Then she focused on him again, stiffening her spine with determination. "We'll fight. You understand that?"

"Yes'm," he mumbled, distracted as earth crumbled under his fingers. He felt the pressure on his foot ease. Cautiously hopeful, he tried shifting it. Maybe . . .

As he wriggled back to straighten the leg, the girl raised the rifle toward his face. Ignoring it, he braced and pulled. His foot jerked free. Leaning back on his elbows, he dragged deep breaths and grinned at the girl. "I reckon I made it."

She nodded, but she didn't seem to be paying him much attention. She was thinking hard and frowning as she did it.

He shot a look toward the lowering sun. "How far is it from here to a place called Gaff's Crossroads?"

"About ten miles." she muttered.

He gave a shake of his head. His foot was throbbing. Not busted, but sore all right. "I sure can't walk no ten miles. Not tonight. Ma'am, if you've decided not to shoot me, I think maybe you owe me a ride into town."

"Huh?"

"In fact, I think you owe me a horse."

"Huh?" she repeated.

He gestured at the dead mare. The girl eyed it. Lowering the rifle, she sighed. "All right, I suppose so."

"A horse?" he grunted incredulously.

She nodded and turned to collect her mount. With a practiced deftness, she stepped up to the sidesaddle and slipped the rifle into the scabbard hanging at the off side. She adjusted her skirt, then heeled the horse toward him. "Get up behind me."

He hauled himself off the ground. The hurt foot complained about taking his weight. Balancing on one leg, he caught the cantle of her saddle. There was a bedroll and war bag lashed behind it. That struck him right curious. He dragged himself up onto the pony's rump. As he settled astride it, she put the animal into a lope.

After a moment he asked conversationally, "This Three-Slash-C is a ranch or something?"

"Yes, a ranch."

"Near to here?"

"Not far."

Tentatively he suggested, "It'll be darkening soon. Maybe you got a place on this ranch where I could bed down tonight, get on into town tomorrow? Maybe you could spare me some eats?"

"We're not going to the ranch," she said in a vague, distracted way. "Don't worry. You'll be taken care of."

He wondered exactly what she meant by that.

CHAPTER 2

Despite the throbbing in his foot and the uncertainties ahead of him, he allowed to himself that the day was still a good one. The pain was a nuisance but it would go away eventually. The uncertainties could be dangerous, but they could be fun too. And although the girl in front of him on the bay wasn't exactly beautiful, she was thoroughly intriguing. He wished she would put the horse into a gallop. Something fast and jolting enough to excuse him grabbing her around the waist. Just to hang on, of course.

But the bay's lope was too easy-riding to give him any excuses, so he kept his hands to himself. And the girl seemed too deep in her own thoughts to make talk, so he contented himself with wondering where the hell they were going and just what he'd gotten into. And whether he might actually be the man she wanted to kill.

They came out of a woods onto the fringes of rolling bottomland. It was a wide basin, broken by jutting slopes and ridges, flecked with patches of brush, and bright-tinted green with new grass. The scents that rose off it were lush and good. Real fine cattle land, he thought. Three-Slash-C land?

The girl had been relaxing as they rode. She handled her mount as if she'd been raised to horseback and took pleasure in riding. He had been mulling around for some kind of innocent comments that might get her to talking about herself when she spoke up so suddenly that she startled him.

"You *have* to have a name," she said.

He grinned, glad she was at ease enough now to concern herself with trivial things. Making his voice as blank as he could, he asked, "Why?"

"Everyone does. You inherit a name from your fath— from a parent. Everyone has at least one parent."

"Almost everyone," he offered in correction.

"Melchisedec?" She didn't look back at him, but she sounded as if she were smiling.

"Ma'am?"

"Without father, without mother, without descent, having neither beginning of days, nor end of life; but made like unto the Sun of God; abideth a priest continually."

"Huh?" He realized she was quoting. "What's that from?"

"Hebrews."

"Who?"

"Hebrews. In the Bible."

It wasn't often anyone threw Scriptures at him. Sure hadn't anybody ever accused him of being *from* them before. Trying to sound thoughtful and serious, he answered, "Well, I like the part about no end of life, but not the piece about being a priest. I've knowed some priests, and it ain't nothing I'd care for at all."

"Then you're not Melchisedec?" This time the amusement was obvious in her voice.

He liked that. With the tension gone, she seemed capable of laughing easily. Still pretending seriousness, he said, "Not if I got to be a priest for it. No, ma'am."

"Well, you have to be someone. People must call you something."

"Oh, yes'm, they call me a lot of things."

"For instance?"

"Sometimes *Chico,* or *Hey, you there,* or maybe *Gringo.* Sometimes *Loco.*"

She glanced over her shoulder at him. One eyebrow was raised in question. "Loco?"

He nodded.

She knew what it meant all right. With a twisty little smile, she said, "It fits."

"Yes'm," he answered solemnly. It was hard to keep from grinning at her. She waited as if she figured he'd go on and give her a proper kind of name for himself. He considered the idea. It was Ray deVaca who'd tagged him Loco. Might be as good a handle to use as any when Ray came looking for him. *If* Ray came. For a brief, serious moment, he wondered if Ray had made it across the river. Maybe they shouldn't have split up—but if they hadn't maybe they'd both be dead now.

When he failed to give her any other name for himself, she shrugged and smiled. "All right, Loco. What brings you to these parts?"

"Most of the way, a tobiana mare."

"You know what I mean."

"Well, I left out of Mexico and this is where I got to," he sighed. "Might be I'd have got farther if you hadn't shot my horse."

"This is a long way from Mexico." The way she said it implied a question.

He wondered how much it would take to spook her. He didn't really want to, but the temptation was there. He let it out just a little ways. "Yes'm, that's *exactly* what I had in mind."

She caught his meaning all right, and it didn't seem to bother her. She was curious to know more. "With no gear and no gun, eh?"

"I kinda left 'em in Mexico," he owned, amused at the effect a little blank-faced, outright honesty could have when it was used right. Sometimes it could convince an otherwise wary person that he was dealing with a harmless half-wit. Just because he allowed as how he'd run from trouble, she assumed it must be the small kind. He added, "I left there in kind of a hurry."

Satisfied that she understood, she asked, "A señorita?"

"Kind of," he mumbled, letting her think what she chose. It wasn't exactly a lie. There had been a girl mixed up in it. She was the one who'd betrayed them to the *Federales*. *Puta pelada.*

"You *are* loco," Ruth said.

He liked the sound of laughter in her voice. He decided he liked Ruth Caisson altogether. She struck him as a solid-minded woman with a good sense of humor and of self-respect. She was obviously used to being around men, and not only when they were on their best behavior either. She had a notion she was in complete control of the situation right now. Well, that was fine with him. Let her think whatever she pleased, as long as it worked to his advantage.

He figured her for the lone girl in a batch of brothers, or else a first child to a strong-minded father. Maybe she was an only child to one. From her rig and manner, she was lady enough—but not too much.

She had assumed the authority to promise him a horse for the one she'd killed, so she was likely either wife or daughter to the owner of this Three-Slash-C. Used to having hired hands give her respect and loyalty and some spoiling, he reckoned.

The haze in the distance caught his eye. It wasn't mist, but roiling dust. For an instant it puzzled him. He thought of horsemen on the move. Troopers, maybe. That was wrong though. He knew that even before he made out the sounds.

Cattle were bawling, miserable and mad. Men yowled in answer to them. Hoofs milled and clattered and caught other sounds in with them to make a heavy rumbling undertone behind the yelps and bellows.

He grinned as he understood. Sure, it was grass-up time and there'd be cow hunting and calf branding and all kinds of sweat-drenching, backbreaking work to keep hired men busy this time of the year. Likely it was a roundup camp that they were riding into.

When they reached the crest of the rise, someone in the cow camp spotted them and gave a holler of recognition. The girl spurred the bay in response. Snorting, it laid back its ears and dove into a run as hard as if it had been in the middle of a buffalo herd.

Startled, Loco caught his balance before he remembered his thoughts about hanging on. He considered it for

a moment. But that long, lean rider who'd cut away from
the bunched cattle and was heading toward them just might
be the girl's father or husband. So he kept his hands to
himself.

The girl was laughing as she drew rein short of the camp.
The man who rode to meet her grinned behind his mask of
sweat-caked dust. They fell in side-by-side, both horses
ambling, swinging in a circle around the holding ground.
The bay tossed its head, snuffling and snorting complaints
about such a short, unrewarding run.

The long, lean cowhand and his horse were both thoroughly dunned with dust. Loco couldn't tell much about
either one. The horse could have been a dark sorrel or a
bay or even a roan. The man might have been thirty or
forty or something on either side. He was a cowhand,
though, and not a boss. At least not over the girl. Not to
judge by the way he lifted his hat to her and nodded, a
little like a peon to his patron.

"How's it going, Deck?" she asked, still laughing and
a bit breathless.

He lost his trace of a grin. With dark solemnity, he
said, "Kinda short on the tally."

She stopped laughing. "Bad?"

"Kinda," Deck answered.

Loco had a notion that meant *real* bad.

The girl gave a weary sigh. Deck stayed knee to knee
with her as she reined her horse toward the chuck wagon.
He looked at Loco, but he spoke to Ruth. "Who's this?"

"Loco." The edge of teasing amusement was in her
voice again. Halting, she gestured for her passenger to dis-
mount.

He slid off the bay's rump and started to offer the
girl a hand down. But a hard-shelled grayback with a flour
sack wrapped around his middle beat him to it. The coosie
cracked the permanent scowling set of his face to give her
a grin. It showed an assortment of gnarled, brown teeth.
The hand he held up to her was covered with dough.

She accepted the biscuity fingers into her own. Lightly, she stepped down from her saddle. Backstepping out of her way, Loco slumped against the wagon. He kept his face blank and innocent. Half-witted. He was a little amused by the suspicious way Deck eyed him. And a little apprehensive, too.

Frowning, Deck said, *"Loco?"*

"That's what he calls himself," Ruth answered. "I found him over on the Coldwater slopes. With a dead horse."

This time Deck looked at the girl and aimed his words at Loco. "Hunting a job? Ever worked cattle before?"

"Not exactly," Loco mumbled, wondering whether there'd be any advantage in getting a job here. He didn't really want the kind of work they were thinking of. And his bruised foot hurt. As he thought about it, he added, "I've drove some, but never done any cow hunting. I'd be glad to trade some camp chores for eats though."

"A tramp," Deck snorted.

"Probably a petty thief, too," Ruth said. "He *might* be the man the Sheep sent for, but I doubt it. In any case, we ought to keep an eye on him."

"Want me to truss him up and stow him away, Missy?" the cook offered eagerly.

She shook her head. "I don't think that's necessary."

"No trouble, Missy. Be glad to do it for you."

"No, he's not armed and not likely to be dangerous." She sounded like she didn't think he was *capable* of being dangerous. "Just watch out where his fingers might wander. And find a way for him to earn that meal."

"Yessum!" the coosie turned a glittering eye toward Loco. He looked like an old wolf sighting on a young calf.

Loco was sorry for the kind of contempt Ruth Caisson showed, but it wasn't important enough to do anything about. Not right now. And he didn't care much what the others thought as long as they kept thinking he was harmless. Pride might be a fine thing, but a snake that shakes its rattles too much is likely to get its head shot off before

it ever has a chance to use its fangs. And besides, half
the fun was in misleading people without actually lying
to them.

Nodding like a peon, he reached for the bay's reins.
"I'll tend your horse, ma'am."

The coosie swung openhanded. It was a hard, harsh
blow that slapped against Loco's arm with surprising
strength. "You leave Missy's horse alone!"

Loco stopped his own hand before it fisted and drove
toward the cook's gut. The kind of man they took him for
wouldn't fight back. Rubbing his arm, he looked toward
the girl in astonished question.

"Sundance is a rather special horse. I'm particular about
who handles him." There was a hint of apology in her
voice. She smiled.

"I'll tend him, ma'am."

Loco looked at the young cowhand who'd just come
up and spoke. Traces of mud were smeared around the
edges of the boy's fresh-polished face. His cheeks glistened
with water and his hair was soaked, slicked down and
dripping. A brand-new bandana was knotted at his throat.
He had obviously done a hurried job of making himself
as presentable as possible. Glowing, he grinned bashfully
at Ruth.

She turned her smile toward him and handed him the
reins. "Thank you, Ronny."

The wet face became a bright red. The grin stretched
itself from one ear to the other, and unintelligible sounds
scraped around in the boy's throat as he took them from
her hand.

Deck had dismounted. He held out his own reins toward
the boy. He might as well have waited for a cast-iron hitch-
ing post to reach up and take them. The kid was oblivious.
Grunting with disgust, Deck stuffed them into Ronny's
hand.

Seeming unaware that he led more than one horse, the
boy headed away. He bounced with every stride.

Ruth turned her back to Loco, dismissing him from

her attention. Speaking softly and seriously, she asked Deck, "Are the other ranchers all around camp?"

"There's Martin, and Bremen . . ." He began counting them on his fingers as they walked off together. They disappeared around the end of the chuck wagon.

The coosie stepped up to prod Loco in the ribs with a finger stiff as a poker. "There's an ax yonder, and a woods over on the slope, and a whole damn possum belly under the wagon. You got any idea what needs doing?"

"Yeah," Loco muttered. Swinging an ax was a long way from his idea of amusement, but he'd done it before. He supposed once more wouldn't hurt much.

"See that it's *all* you do," the cook snapped after him as he started for the ax.

He nodded, not looking back. His foot hurt enough to lame his stride. It felt like it might have swollen a bit. He wondered if he could find a cool stream somewhere up the slope and soak it. If not, he decided, he'd just stretch out and rest awhile. After all, it'd ruin the notion they all had of him if he actually *worked* at the chore he'd been given, wouldn't it?

The wood lot wasn't very far away, but it seemed a fair distance to walk on the sore foot. It was a distance that no self-respecting *vaquero* would have walked if he'd been able to lay hands on a horse. Loco was mumbling to himself in Spanish by the time he got there.

He found a runlet of icy water and settled himself on the ground beside it, crossing his hurt leg over his knee. His boot looked odd, sort of naked, without the big Mexican spur hung off the heel. It hadn't seemed to matter much, back when he'd traded the spurs for a decent meal in that *calabozo*. He hadn't expected to have a chance to use them again. And the officials hadn't agreed with his idea that a man was entitled to at least one decent meal before he faced a firing squad. Now, though, he missed the spurs. On horseback, he'd felt strange trying to signal the animal without them. It hadn't responded very well to his bare boot heels at first, either. Walking, he missed

the balance of them. And the happy music they'd made.
They'd been a fine, handsome pair of hooks, fitting for a
fine, handsome pair of boots.

Tugging and pulling at the boot didn't seem to be working at all. It just hurt. His ankle was swollen for sure.
With a shrug, he gave it up. Even if he'd had a knife, he
wouldn't have wanted to cut the leather. More than the
spurs, the boots were something special.

He'd never had decent boots before them, never a pair
someone else hadn't worn for a long while first. But back
after the first time he'd worked in a cattle drive into Mexico, he'd had *mucho dinero* in his pocket and he'd decided
on what he wanted. He'd bought leather suited for a
charro's use, and the *artesano de cuero* had built his boots
to order, fitting them carefully to his feet. The man had
worked for perfection. He'd parted with the finished boots
like a man sending his own children off into the world for
the first time. Loco had promised that if he ever came to
Guadalajara again, he'd stop in and let the *artesano* know
how they were getting along. A man could wear boots like
that and care for them, but he couldn't cut them up if he
had any alternative at all.

Limping, Loco hunted a spot that suited him. He chose
a patch of sunlight where he could sprawl and keep an
eye on the camp without being particularly noticeable from
it. Setting down the ax, he lowered himself gently to the
ground and tucked his hands under his head.

What was Ruth Caisson's problem, he wondered.
Likely something to do with the cattle tallying short. Rustling, maybe. Who or what were the *Sheep* she'd mentioned
—the ones who'd sent for someone—and who had they
sent for? Why did Ruth want to kill whoever it was?

And did he want himself a hand in her troubles, or
would it be better to eat his meal, collect the promised
nag first thing in the morning, and light out? He grinned
at that thought. There wasn't any question. He knew
himself well enough to know that he'd hang around at least
until he found out what was going on in this basin. He

couldn't just walk off and leave that big hunk of curiosity unsatisfied. Especially not when there was a woman like Ruth Caisson involved.

The sun was seriously considering disappearing behind the western ridges. It hung over them, poised in deep thought, washing its long light pleasantly over him. The scents of spring were fresh and lush. Things buzzed and chittered in the brush. And distance subdued the racket of the roundup camp into a sort of murmur. It was right pleasant listening to all those waddies hard at work.

Closing his eyes, he remembered the first time he'd gone droving cattle. That time he'd known for sure that the man he hired to owned the beefs. There had been other times when he'd had his doubts. They had paid better. The first time, though, it had been hard, hard work for damn small pay. Too many of the jobs he'd worked at had been. He'd long since had his fill of sweating out his soul so that some other man could stuff a gut with oysters and wine on the profits. Now, he picked his bosses carefully and never offered his soul out for hire. Now, he worked of his own will, for a man of his own choosing, or he didn't work at all.

He had a notion Ruth Caisson would do for a boss. But he wanted to know just what work it was she needed done, and why, before he made any final decision.

Lead spanged the earth close to his elbow.

With a start, he rolled onto his belly. There was no gun to grab for. Feeling naked, he lifted his head slightly to hunt the source of the shot.

The coosie was standing down there by the chuck wagon holding a rifle. Knowing he'd caught Loco's attention, he deliberately levered up another shell and lifted the gun to his shoulder again in a gesture of threat.

With a disgusted sigh, Loco got to his feet and picked up the ax.

CHAPTER 3

As Loco dumped the load of wood beside the wagon, the cook hove up and growled, "That'll about pay for the ca'tridge I had to waste wakening you. I hope you ain't expecting vittles for it, too."

"Hell," Loco muttered, scowling sideways at him, "s'pose you reload your damn cartridge and I'll take this wood and stick it back on the trees, and we can call the whole thing even."

"Start sassing me, boy, and you'll get a skillet flattened on your head." With that, the cook turned his back and tromped toward the fire pit.

Grinning, Loco began stuffing the wood into the possum belly under the wagon. The sky was darkening fast now, and it had been a long time since he'd eaten. The scents of woodsmoke and food cooking stirred juices in his mouth almost faster than he could swallow.

He was aware, without looking, that the cook was busy at something on the tailboard of the wagon. Among the aromas, he picked out cinnamon. Hot apple pie, he thought hopefully. As the cook headed to the fire pit again, he straightened up from his wood-loading and stepped toward the tailboard to check.

The pie tins were lined up along it, all with the sweet dried-apple filling in them. A couple already had their raw crusts on. Dough was spread out for more.

He dipped two fingers into an open one, scooping up some filling to sample. It was delicious. Likely the ornery old buzzard was a damned good cook. It'd be a welcome change from cornmeal and chilies.

The next thought burst full-blown into his mind. He

reached into his pocket for the shriveled pepper that was left of his own stores. As he crumbled it between his fingers over one open pie, he hoped that wasn't the pie Ruth Caisson would get. Well, if it was, that was her bad luck. Just the chance she took messing around a men's camp and eating their chuck. He stirred the crushed pepper into the filling with his fingers. Ducking back to the woodpile, he thoughtlessly started to lick them. As his tongue touched them, he flinched. *Hot* apple pie all right. One of those pies sure wasn't exactly delicious any more. Whistling softly, he finished loading the possum belly.

By the time the men came drifting in for the meal, it was completely dark and there were recollections of snow in the winds that blew down the slopes. A cluster of campfires made a warm, bright circle beside the wagon, though.

Loco noticed with amusement that every cowhand had found time and strength enough to scrub his face and slick his hair. A couple had dug up fresh shirts. And one showed definite signs of having hurriedly shaved with a dull razor in cold water. Miss Caisson's visit to the camp was evidently a very important occasion.

The man she came into the firelight with wasn't Deck. Not any common cowhand from the look of him. He was a tall, stockily built stud dressed in dusty range clothes, but his bearing and the possessive way his hand rested on the girl's arm said he was a boss. One of those ranchers she'd mentioned before, Loco supposed.

A couple of the cowboys dragged a good-sized log up by one of the campfires and put blankets on it to make a seat for the girl. They hauled over a keg to serve her as a table. Thanking them graciously, she seated herself, and the stud sat down at her right. Other men with the air of ranchers rather than hired hands bunched up around her.

Loco watched them light into their food like men who'd done a day's work. They probably had, he told himself. Just because a man owned a ranch didn't necessarily mean he didn't work too. Some ranchers sweated every bit as much as their hired men. Some small ones didn't even have hired men. These ranchers all looked like they'd been busy in the cow hunt themselves. He counted that strongly in their favor.

Falling in with the cowboys, he helped himself to a tin plate and piled it high. There was blanket steak with rich brown gravy, prairie oysters on the side, beans and biscuits and fry, stewed tomatoes out of airtights, several kinds of fruit preserves, and both sorghum and store sugar for sweetening. An impressive mess of eats, especially after weeks of not much more than slimy cornmeal and greasy, overspiced beans.

He settled himself as close to the bunch of ranchers as he could without being conspicuous, and began to eat, listening at the same time.

The one who was speaking was a wiry, sharp-eyed, middle-aged hawk of a man with a face made out of old boot leather. It was decorated with a lush mustache and thick mane that had begun to gray. He looked like flint and steel. But he spoke mildly. "I disagree, Martin. If the Sheep really are bringing in a killer, and we make a move against them, it'll be pure war. We don't want a war in this basin."

"If they're bringing in a killer, we'll have war whether we want it or not!" the stud at Ruth's right answered. He sounded like he'd been simmering a long while and was ready now to boil. "We've got to do *something*. We can't go on like we have been. We'll all be busted within a year if we do."

"They've already killed once," Ruth put in.

"You don't know as how it was the Sheep who did it," a rusty-looking scarecrow of a man said. "You don't even *know* he was murdered."

She snapped, "What else could have happened to him?"

"She's right," Martin said, his hand on her arm again. "What else could have happened? We all knew John Caisson and the kind of man he was. When a man like that rides out and never comes back, it *has* to be murder. Backshooting."

"It could have been a cat, or his horse could have fallen, or . . ." the hawk began.

Martin interrupted. "Like hell! We'd have found him. Somebody killed him and hid the body. You know that, Bremen. It couldn't have been anything else."

"I don't know," Bremen answered with a shrug. "I'm only asking one thing. Just *wait*. See what the Sheep do and whether there really is a hired killer. That rumor may be all wind."

"It could be that bastard Ruth brought in." Martin shot a glance toward Loco. "He's Mexican, isn't he?"

"He says he isn't. He doesn't impress me as a killer, Mart. He doesn't even have a gun," Ruth said.

Bremen grunted, "He's just some tramp."

"How do you know?" Martin snapped at him.

"I don't. Not for sure." He sounded reluctant to admit it.

"You know one thing for sure," Martin said. The argument seemed to be mostly between him and Bremen. "You know that since those nesters moved in we've all been losing cattle. And not just a few head beefed here and there for their tables, either. Somebody's been marketing *our* critters and it ain't us. You *know* that."

"And you know my father's dead," Ruth added.

Bremen nodded, but he said, "If we attack them, there's bound to be war."

"You want to keep on raising beef for them to profit on until you're flat broke?"

"Yeah, what about it?" one of the others piped up.

"I've still got some capital," Bremen offered. "I can advance a few more loans."

"I'm over my head to you now. If I sign one more piece of paper, I might as well give my place away," the rusty scarecrow grumbled. Others nodded and muttered in tones of agreement.

"Suppose we talk to them?" the fat one in the bunch suggested.

"My father went to talk to them. He never came back," Ruth said.

The scarecrow agreed with fatty. "We ought to talk before we do anything. It ain't fair lest you give'm warning."

"They've been warned," Martin answered him.

They kept going on the same way, exchanging a lot of words but adding nothing more to what Loco'd collected so far. As he listened to them, he kept an eye on the pies setting to cool on the tail gate of the wagon. The first one that got cut was obviously not the hot one. That was just as well. Ruth and several of the ranchers were served out of it. The second one didn't cause any unexpected stir either. It wasn't till a bandy buck in a fresh shirt got himself the first wedge of the third pie that anything interesting happened.

The bandy took a big mouthful, clomped his jaw shut on it, and suddenly exploded. Unchawed pieces of apple sprayed the fire and scattered down the clean shirt front. Snapping to his feet like a tripped bear trap, he charged toward the coosie. The words he began to spew impressed Loco as fair expressive for cussing limited to just one language.

It disrupted the ranchers' discussion. And everything else in the camp. There was sudden silence.

The bandy became aware of it. He caught himself an instant before he reached the cook. Aghast, he realized that he was putting on his show in front of Ruth Caisson. He halted so hard that he reared back on his haunches like a spade-bitted horse. His face turned an even darker shade than it had at a taste of the pie. Loco couldn't be sure by the glare of the firelight, but he expected it was a sort of plum purple.

Try as he might, he couldn't keep a grin off his face as he watched the bandy wheel and gallop into the darkness.

Blankly bewildered, the coosie glanced around for some sort of explanation.

All of the men were very aware of Ruth Caisson's presence. The laughter was frozen in their throats. Their faces twisted in mixed amusement and embarrassment. It was Deck who finally spoke. "Something wrong with the pie?"

"Not with *my* pie!" the cook snarled. He slammed his plate down on the tail gate and grabbed a knife. Hacking himself a slab of pie, he sampled it.

Loco decided the old man must have a will of cast iron. From the look of his face, it wasn't his mouth that was metal, but he managed to chaw and then to swallow down the whole bite. After a long, long moment of working up enough juices to flush his tongue, he gulped a few times and rasped. "Chili . . ."

He turned slowly, his eyes scanning the circle of faces that peered at him. He settled on Loco and added one hoarse word—*"Mexican."*

Loco saw it coming all right. He was on his feet by the time the charging coosie rammed into him. It was like being hit headlong by a steam engine. He felt his hurt ankle buckle.

Somebody shouted, "Timber-r-r!"

Loco hit ground on his back, with the coosie piled on top of him. Thoughts about being watched by a lady didn't stop the old man at all. They didn't even slow him down. Neither did his gnarled age. Even as the ground slammed against Loco's back, the old man's fingers were locking onto his throat. The thumbs caught him under the Adam's apple and shoved in, digging deep.

Along with the wild urge to save himself from being strangled, Loco felt an instant of admiration for this vinegaroon. He didn't waste much time contemplating it, though. He got his own hands up, between the cook's arms. With all the strength he could manage in such an awkward position, he rammed his forearms against the cook's, slamming outward. It broke the grip.

The cook had been propped on the hands that he pressed into Loco's throat. As they were knocked from under him, he flopped forward.

Loco grabbed, grappling him around the body. Hugging him close, he tried to roll. He wanted a lot to get on top of the heap. But as he flung his arms around the cook, he discovered that the old man had made a mistake. One that could have been fatal, if Loco'd wanted it to be. The cook had a knife sheathed on the back of his belt.

Loco let go his hug and wrapped his fingers around the hilt. Even as the old man realized that the bear grip was broken, Loco had the point of the blade pricking into his brisket.

The coosie understood quick enough. Loco could feel the flash of a shudder that ran through him.

"Get off me," Loco said softly. He drew the knife back slightly, holding it poised in threat.

The cook rose to his knees. He darted a glance at Loco's hand and saw the blade aimed to drive into his gut. Obediently he got to his feet and backstepped.

Loco swung up to a slight crouch, the knife still ready to strike. It looked as natural in his hand as fangs in a diamondback's mouth.

His back was to the circle of men around the fire. He realized that. And, as the cook glanced past him, he realized the old man had intentionally maneuvered him into the position. Again he was aware of a flash of admiration. At the same time, something that felt like a gun muzzle rammed him in the spine.

"Drop it, mister!" The shaky young voice belonged to the kid who'd taken care of Ruth's horse. Loco recognized it easily enough. The kid was dumb, inexperienced, and a fool. To judge from his face, the cook had the same thought. But it was all happening too quickly for the old man to offer any warning.

Letting the knife slide out of his hand, Loco spun on one foot.

He wheeled away from the muzzle of the rifle that the kid had stupidly touched to him. His side slapped against the barrel as the boy jerked the trigger.

Through the sudden roar and haze of powder smoke, he saw Ronny wince in surprise. Not fear. It was too quick. The kid didn't have time to understand that he should be afraid. Loco's hands had already closed on the gun and were wrenching it out of his grip.

The cook might have tried to help, but Loco had the rifle free of Ronny's hold. He was turning again, back-stepping. He got them all—the boy, the cook, and the startled cowhands who'd watched without doing anything about it—in front of him.

Again, he felt an admiration for the *cocinero*. The old man pitched his voice low so it wouldn't carry, but he mingled the best of Texas brasada talk with highly imaginative Mexican, and he did it with soul-searing sincerity.

Loco grinned. He saw the girl approaching. The cook didn't. The shocked boy, who hadn't yet figured out how he'd lost the upper hand, was the one who noticed her. Hoarsely, he gasped, "Miss Ruth!"

The coosie stopped in mid-word. He glared at Loco as if her presence within earshot was his fault too.

"Is it over?" she asked.

"If they're willing, I am," Loco said huskily. His throat felt a mite sore where the cook's thumbs had dug in.

She looked questioningly toward the old man. Abashed, he scanned the faces of his audience and grumbled, "He'll eat every damn bit of that pizened pie afore it's over."

"I'll eat as much of it as you do," Loco answered.

The cook snapped back, "Dollar says you *can't!*"

"I don't have a dollar."

"I'll cover it," one of the cowhands shouted.

The coosie scurried to get the rest of the pie. Loco handed the rifle over to Ruth. He walked toward the chuck wagon, licking his lips. But not in anticipation.

Moods could change quicker than lightning could flash. There was no sense of trouble or threat in the camp now. The cowhands were busy making bets, completely distracted by the prospect of a contest. And Ruth was watching it all with a gentle amusement. She didn't bet. Loco wondered where she'd have put her money, if she did.

An intent silence blanketed the camp as the contest began. Men watched, grimacing in sympathy and gulping coffee, but not speaking lest they distract the pie eaters. Within the first few bites, Loco took the lead.

From what he'd seen of the world, if there was a way to cheat at a gambling game, somebody had found it already, and everybody was doing it. He had no objections at all to a little honest cheating when it was to his own advantage—even at pie-eating.

He fell a couple of chaws behind, swallowed hard, gagged, and lost more ground. The odds changed, and there was a hushed whispering as men made more wagers. Then silence again.

The pie was pretty terrible stuff. Even for a man who'd had a lot of practice putting down chili-hot eats it was a mouthful. And the combination of flavors—the apples and cinnamon and sweetening mixed with the spice—was something awful.

He was way behind when, with a snort of triumph, the coosie snatched up the last fragment of the mess.

The men who'd made bets grumbled and chortled as they settled up. Loco grinned to himself. After all, *he* hadn't had any money in the game.

Scowling happily, the coosie washed out his mouth with scalding black coffee and tallied up the paper promises he'd won on his own bets. There was no resentment or anger in the quick look he darted at Loco. He was satisfied.

But Loco had a feeling Ruth Caisson wasn't. She rejoined the ranchers, palavering some more, but she kept glancing thoughtfully toward him. And each glance seemed a little darker than the one before.

As he helped himself to coffee, Loco considered the things he'd learned here this evening. Trouble was going to bust loose in this basin right soon. Big, messy trouble with the stink of killing in it. And he knew he'd be mixed up in it, no matter what.

He felt certain that the man the Sheep were rumored to have sent for was Ray deVaca.

CHAPTER 4

The sun hadn't shown itself yet, but the first glow of its coming was in the air. Only the coosie and the wrangler were up and around when Loco woke. The scent of cooking coffee rode the morning breeze and tickled his nose. He decided it might be worth-while to get up. Rolling out of the ragged soogan he'd managed to borrow, he sat up stiffly.

His foot still felt sore, there was a dull aching in his head, and his mouth tasted like somebody had burnt a hairy hide in it and not bothered to sweep out the ashes. Otherwise he felt pretty good. Standing, he stretched and thought wishfully about hot baths and skillful barbers. Was this Gaff's Crossroads a big-enough town to have either, he wondered. Well, in any case, he didn't have any coin in his poke. And he wasn't at all sure he was still heading for Gaff's Crossroads. The troubled gray eyes of the girl were very much in his mind.

As he headed for the coffeepot, the coosie shot him a dark scowl. He ignored it. Helping himself to a cup full of the thick black brew, he looked across the fire at the wrangler.

The kid was perched on the log that had been Ruth's dinner chair. Sipping his own coffee, he watched Loco curiously over the brim of the cup. His eyes were the same color as the coffee, and his face almost as dark. He didn't look old enough yet to be concerned about barbers himself.

Loco grinned at him. He grinned back, shy but friendly enough, so Loco went on around the fire and sat down beside him.

"I reckon you're the horse boss around here?"

The kid looked sideways at him, not sure how to answer that. Likely nobody'd ever suggested he was *boss* of anything before. His grin spread even broader with bashful pride as he considered the idea.

"Been around these parts a while, I s'pose?" Loco tried. He hoped he could get the kid talking. Sometimes young 'uns had a way of knowing what was going on around them.

The boy gave him a nod in reply.

"Then you'd know these *Sheep* everybody's talking about?"

That seemed to startle the kid, maybe even frighten him a bit. He gave a hard shake of his head and gazed intently into his coffee cup.

"You know *about* them, though?"

The kid gave another curt nod.

"They keep sheep, huh?"

"No, sir," he mumbled. "They the Lord's folk."

"Huh?"

The boy spoke slowly, without looking up. "That's what they say, mister. Bossman there, he says him and his people belong to the Lord and if we mess with 'em, the Lord's gonna get mad at us. He says if our beef disappear, it's the Lord's doing and not his."

"What do *you* think?" Loco asked him.

He squirmed and gave a solemn shake of his head. "I don't think nothing. It ain't my place to do no thinking. I only just hope ain't nothing happens to none of my horses."

He was troubled and scared, Loco thought. Likely torn between loyalty to his own boss and a fearful respect for the people who claimed to belong to the Lord. He asked, "What brand do you ride?"

At that the boy grinned again. "Missy Caisson's."

Loco returned the grin. "She's a good boss?"

"Yessir!" For a moment the happy pride held on the

boy's face. Then it faded. He sipped at his coffee and eyed Loco sideways again. "Some says you're the Mexican, mister. Some says you belong to them Sheep and not to us."

"I don't belong to anybody."

"Not at all?"

"No."

He studied on that awhile. "Missy needs more help," he suggested. "Maybe you'd come work for her."

"Maybe," Loco allowed. "You tell me some more about these Sheep."

"I don't know nothing, only they came here about a year back. Mister Caisson, he didn't mind none. He said they wasn't gonna hurt nothing. Then the fall cow hunt, the beefs tally up short, and everybody says the Sheep took 'em. Mister Caisson, he went out, gonna go talk to them, only he didn't never come back. Now everybody says they gonna be bad trouble. I don't know."

"What happened when Mister Caisson disappeared? Did anybody do anything?"

"They looked for him. Didn't find no trace of him. Some says it's like the ground swallowed him up. Mister Martin, he says the Sheep killed him and buried him. He wanted them to go run out them Sheep, only Mister Bremen, he says, 'Wait.' All the time, he says, 'Wait.' He made everybody wait till now, but the cowboys says the tally's bad short again and they ain't gonna wait much longer. Says them Sheep is hiring killers, gonna make a war."

Loco nodded. It was all pretty much the same story he'd overheard at the fire last night.

"Mister Shepherd, he says it's the Lord's doing," the boy added thoughtfully.

"Who's Mister Shepherd?"

"He's the bossman over there. He says he's the Lord's Shepherd and them Sheep is all his flock."

"They call themselves *Sheep?*" Loco asked incredulously.

"No, sir. It was Mister Martin took to calling 'em that. Then everybody done it. Only now Mister Martin says they really a flock of wolves."

"Mister Martin seems to be a bit of a curly wolf himself."

Nodding, the kid grinned, then asked, "You gonna come work for Missy?"

"I just might."

The boy finished off his coffee. As he got to his feet, he said, "You come work for Missy and I'll pick you out a good string of horses. Not no sorebacks and rockheads, huh, mister?"

"Yeah, *amigo*."

" *'Migo?*"

"Friend," Loco explained.

" *'Migo*," the kid repeated, savoring the word and liking it. Loco watched him hurry off toward the *remuda* and wondered about the trouble with the Sheep. He wondered about Martin, too. Ruth Caisson was too special a girl for a stud like Martin. Maybe if there was a war the rancher would do her a favor and get himself killed off.

The tip of the sun had edged itself up over the rim. Before long it would be blazing away. Men were up and around in the camp now, and breakfast was about ready. As he sipped his coffee, Loco watched the wagon where the girl had bedded. In a while, she came around the far end of it, headed for the coffeepot. She had a cup in her hand.

"Morning, ma'am," he smiled, rising to tilt the pot for her. She nodded in reply, but her face was hard set and her glance at him cold. Wordlessly, she took the full cup and turned back toward the wagon. She disappeared around the end of it.

Loco didn't like it. And he didn't like the way the foreman appeared from behind the wagon a minute later. Deck strode a straight line directly toward him.

"Miss Ruth wants to see you," the foreman said. His face was as grim as the girl's had been.

"She promised me a horse," Loco muttered, tossing his cup into the wreck box as he fell in at Deck's side. He didn't think this had anything to do with the horse. There was an apprehensive tension along his spine. As if Deck were leading him into a blind corral.

The ranchers were bunched up together on the far side of the wagon waiting. Martin stood next to Ruth, his hand possessively on her arm again.

Loco halted, sidestepping to put his back to the wagon. It was almost an instinctive move. He scanned the faces that looked like thunderclouds about to bust loose, and he knew his hand was about to be called. Hell, he'd meant to play this one his own way, in his own good time.

"Look here, you . . ." Martin began angrily.

"Mart," the girl interrupted. She put her hand on his, as if to hold him back by it. "Let me."

"But, Ruth . . ."

"Let me," she repeated, and this time it sounded more like an order than a request.

Bremen started, "Ruth, this isn't anything for a woman. You shouldn't even be here. . . ."

Insistently, she interrupted again. "Let me."

They yielded to her. She took a step forward, almost pulling free of Martin's grip. But he moved quickly to stay beside her.

Loco gave her a blank and questioning look.

She wasn't buying it though. Her voice was heavy with accusation. "You're too quick, Loco. You're not as dumb as you look."

"I'm sure glad of that," he grinned.

She wasn't willing to be put off or amused. Sternly, she said, "I want the truth."

"Nothing I've told you wasn't true."

"No!" She gave a shake of her head in denial. "You aren't what you've led us to believe."

"Sometimes people lie to each other. Sometimes they lie to themselves and blame it on each other."

"What's that supposed to mean?" Martin snapped.

Ruth's hand touched his again, silently asking him to
stay out of it. This, it seemed, was between her and Loco.
At least she seemed to think of it that way. Something
personal.

Loco read it in her face. She'd trusted him. Now she felt
he'd betrayed that trust. He told her, "Not one thing I've
said to you wasn't true. If you have some other ideas
about me, you got 'em for yourself."

"You're talking around the barn."

"But I'm telling the truth," he answered with a shrug.

He wasn't reaching her though. She looked like she
wanted to spit in his eye. Taking a deep breath, she held
her voice coldly steady. "We've discussed it and we think
you *are* the man the Sheep sent for."

"No, ma'am."

"If we're wrong," she went on, "we'll apologize. But until we can be certain, you're going to be our guest. Whether
you like it or not."

"I got no objections. The food's good here."

"Damned right you got no objections," Martin grunted.
He gestured for Deck. "Just to make sure, we're going to
keep you hobbled."

Deck tugged a pigging string from under his belt.

Sighing, Loco leaned his shoulders against the side of
the wagon. He put all of his weight on his good foot.

"Cross your hands," Deck said, stepping up to him.

He lifted his hands obediently. He held them close to
his chest. The foreman took another step toward him,
reaching out with the pigging string. Loco's face was
slackly submissive.

He grinned suddenly as he slammed his right knee up
between Deck's legs. Gasping with pain, the foreman
doubled from the waist. Loco's right hand rammed up
under his jaw, snapping his head back. His left hand caught
Deck's right wrist. With a twisting shove he turned the
startled man full around, face toward the ranchers. He
brought the caught arm up behind Deck's back, the hand
high between the shoulder blades.

Deck squirmed, struggling helplessly against the grip that could easily wrench his arm bones out of joint. Loco held him with his left hand. His right wrapped onto the butt of the gun holstered on the foreman's hip. There was nothing Deck could do about it. Through set teeth, he snarled, "I'll kill you."

"You think so, huh?" Loco pressed the muzzle of the gun against the man's waist. Over Deck's shoulder, he looked at the surprised, bewildered, frustrated, and irate faces of the ranchers who'd thought they had him prisoner.

The sharp sounds of that moment of scuffling had brought cowhands around to see what was happening. They made a wide half-circle behind the ranchers. Several men had gone for their own sidearms. But Loco had the wagon at his back and Deck full in front of him. A good-enough shield to keep any of them from getting notions about shooting. He was safe enough sandwiched in here. The question now was how to get himself out safely.

He looked at Ruth Caisson. "You folks got a hell of a way of treating *guests*."

"You liar!" she snapped at him. The sense of it being a personal matter, between the two of them, was still there. That pleased him.

With hurt innocence, he said, "Man comes along minding his own business. Gets shot at. Gets his horse slaughtered. Gets jumped twice. All on account of how he dresses."

"You're the Mexican," Martin said.

"Unh ugh," Loco shook his head.

"Then what the devil are you?"

"Nothing *you'd* understand, mister. Far as it matters to you, I'm just some stranger happened by and you've been making trouble for ever since. I *ain't* the hired killer you think I am, but I'm getting damned tempted to be. If you're as fair-minded with these nesters as you have been with me, maybe they *need* gun help." Looking toward

Ruth, he added mockingly, "You promised me a horse for the one you killed. Or did that just happen to be a lie?"

Anger flared in her eyes. Her lips framed a word that she didn't voice. He could guess what it was, though. Shaping righteous shock on his face, he shook his head sadly.

She blushed. It was fun to see. The color rose up her throat and spread on her cheeks. And that seemed to embarrass her as much as his mockery had. She glared at him as if she could take great pleasure in shooting him now.

Suddenly he was sorry. Teasing a woman might be fine sport, but there were times and places when it shouldn't be pushed. This girl had troubles that were plenty real. He couldn't expect her to appreciate his twisted humor at the moment.

Seriously he said, "I swear I'm not the hired killer you've been looking for."

Tiny creases grooved into her forehead as she struggled with her anger. It was as though she really *wanted* to believe him. But she needed more proof than just his word.

"Let Deck go," she said quietly, almost as if it were a suggestion.

It would likely be a fool thing to do, he thought. He could end up either shooting or getting himself hog-tied if he did. Ropes, shackles, locks, imprisonment of any kind galled the spirit. Even walls and roofs sometimes oppressed a man's soul. But as things were right now, it was a standoff that he couldn't hold forever. And someone always had to make the first move of good faith—or of surrender.

Good faith, he told himself hopefully. Keeping his gaze on the girl, he loosed his grip on the foreman's arm. At the same time he shoved the man away from him.

It wasn't expected. Deck lurched forward, falling. He caught himself on his hands and knees. Rising, he gripped the arm that must have hurt plenty now and faced Loco.

The gun was still in Loco's hand, cocked but not raised. Deck eyed it, his burning fury held in check by it. Tensely he said, "I'll kill you."

"No!" Ruth snapped. "Nobody's going to kill anybody around here." She spoke toward Deck, but she was looking at Loco. He knew she was asking him a question.

He nodded in reply and saw the flash of relief in her face. This time she'd accepted his word.

"Ruth . . ." Martin began.

But once more she pulled rein on him. She laid her hand on his and looked up into his face. Her eyes were a mixture of pleading and ordering. Huskily, she said, "Let me, Mart."

Loco could see Martin melting at the caress of her voice. Hell, he felt shimmery around the edges from it himself. A man would be hard put to keep a woman like that under control, he thought. Be fun to try.

Martin seemed almost to shrink physically under her gaze. He yielded silently. The other ranchers stood unspeaking. There was bewilderment in most of the faces as they watched. They didn't seem to quite understand. Or to be willing to take the lead. At least none were willing to fight Ruth Caisson for it. She was in command.

Turning her attention to her foreman, she squared her shoulders. She knew her position. Authority rang in her tone. "Deck, is this a cow hunt or a Sunday social?"

"Huh?"

She gestured toward the cowhands watching the show. "Do you suppose there's *anybody* out working?"

Deck drew himself up and looked at his men with a silent snarl. They, too, began to melt, but in a different way. Suddenly they were oozing away, finding themselves very busy.

"What about the Sheep?" Martin asked, his voice too loud and taut. "Are we gonna do something about them or not?"

"Let it wait awhile," Bremen suggested mildly.

Martin shook his head. "I dunno nothing about this Mexican, but I do know my tally's short. We've *got* to do something."

"We will," Ruth said with a sigh. "But right now, I'd like to have breakfast."

"Of course, my dear." Martin gave the words a condescending twist, trying to imply that he was holding the reins and simply humoring the girl. As he put his hand on her arm again, she smiled at him. Loco got the impression that she would have preferred to laugh at him.

She started to turn away. Then she looked back over her shoulder at Loco. He lifted an eyebrow in question.

"Go ahead!" she snapped. "Take a horse. Get out. Do whatever you want to!"

CHAPTER 5

Loco took his horse and went.

Since nobody offered any objections, he took his pick of the *remuda*—a coyote dun geld that the wrangler recommended highly. The kid dug him up a bridle, but there wasn't anything in the line of a spare saddle around the camp. He considered going back up the slopes for the old kack he'd left on the carcass of the tobiana, but once he was astride the dun, he decided its bare back was more comfortable than the battered old hulk had been.

Waving good-bye to the kid, he nudged the dun's flanks with his heels and headed off to hunt Gaff's Crossroads.

It was another fresh and fair spring day. Even saddle-less, he figured he'd done well enough for himself in the cow camp. He had a far better horse now than he'd had before, and a paper saying he was legally entitled to it. He'd gotten a good meal. And he was armed now. Deck's revolver was tucked into the waistband of his britches. In all the hubbub, it seemed to have been forgotten. At least no one had asked him to give it back. And he hadn't seen any point in volunteering it. After all, it wasn't exactly theft, he figured. More like the spoils of war.

Now all he needed was a saddle, a couple of knives, a belt and sheath for the gun, spurs, and a hat. And some coin in his pocket.

Whistling cheerfully, he hunted up the wagon road the wrangler had described. It took him over hummocky grassland patched with outcrops of rock, spates of gravel, and occasional fuzzy clumps of brush. Topping a scrub-crusted rise, he sighted the red flag of the store.

It had to be Gaff's Crossroads, even though he could

only see the one set of wagon tracks that he followed. There were maybe half a dozen buildings sparsely scattered around on a slope. No two were alike. The thing under the flag seemed to have begun as a simple one-room cabin, but had taken the gout. Warts and swellings of additional rooms stuck out on all sides of it. The plank growth at the front overwhelmed the old cabin. Chickens wandered around it, a hog and a hound sprawled amiably together in the sun by the front door, and a picketed goat nibbled garbage in the back.

Loco drew rein at the hitch rail. Sliding off the dun, he glanced back. He wondered who it was who'd followed him from the cow camp.

When he shoved open the door, an attached thong jangled a sleigh bell. The sound was sharp and jarring within the twilight darkness of the cavernous store. Not much light managed to seep through the small, filthy panes of glass set into the end walls. It barely gave shape to heaps of objects bulking in the room. He paused just inside the doorway, waiting for his eyes to adjust. The place smelled mostly of leather, harness oil, whiskey, and goat.

He heard creaking and footfalls. Then dim light framed the man who pulled aside the blanket hanging in a doorway between the store and the cabin. He came into the room, dropping the blanket and almost disappearing into the shadows. Loco watched his faint form weave through the piles of merchandise to a table under one window.

The man struck a sulphur match. It flared, stinking and showing Loco a face as gaunt as stripped bone. Once the storekeeper put the match to a lamp wick, the room brightened. Rows of tins and jars appeared on shelves along the walls. Blankets and harnesses hung down from the rafters. The shapeless heaps on the floor became barrels and boxes and full sacks.

The storekeeper rested his elbows on the table that served for a counter, eyed Loco and grunted.

Stepping up, Loco asked, "Are you Gaff?"

"I'm Cullough. There isn't any Gaff," the man said, his

voice dry and rattly as gravel in a tin pan.

"Ain't any cross roads either, is there?"

"You're an observant man."

Loco nodded, glancing at the tapped kegs behind the counter. "And a thirsty one. You got drinking likker?"

In answer, Cullough drew pale liquid from one keg into a cup and shoved it toward him. It smelled raw. It tasted like snake juice. Searing Loco's gullet, it hit bottom with a hot thud.

He wiped his mouth with the back of his hand, then asked, "Has there been a *hombre* in here looking for me yet? He's a . . ."

"No. Been nobody in here looking for anybody. Or nothing else."

"He'll come. When he does, you tell him I'm around."

"Sure. That's two bits for the whiskey."

Loco grinned slightly. A little sadly. "I guess you're gonna have to start a tally for me."

"You ain't got money?"

"Right."

"Work around here?"

"No."

"Work anywhere?"

He shook his head.

"I shoulda knowed," Cullough grumbled wearily. "Lord, I shoulda learned by now, never pour till I've clinked the coin."

"You're new at this business, huh?" Loco asked amiably.

The storekeeper shrugged and sighed. "I've been in the business awhile now, but I sure ain't had much experience. Customers rush in here as eager as they would to a lazaret. You wouldn't want to work off that two bits, would you, Buster?"

"No, not *work*. Tell you what, though. You remember to give my friend my message when he comes in, and he'll pay you. Tell him his crazy friend said to give you the two bits."

"Write it down for him." He shoved a ruled pad and the stub of a pencil toward Loco.

"Wouldn't do no good."

"Can't he read?"

"Not *my* writing."

"Hell," Cullough mumbled, sounding too tired and discouraged to really care.

"Things pretty bad around here?" Loco asked him. He nodded.

"I heard there was a settlement of farmers. Ought to be customers enough to keep up a store like this."

"Sure, there *ought* to be. Man who sold me this poke said there would be. But them—hell, that bunch at the settlement don't buy nothing. You never seen a worse hard-scrabble, penny-pinching bunch of hymn-hollerers than them Sheep."

"That so?"

"Ranchers, cowboys, settlers, farmers—basin's full of 'em. Shake the whole lot over a barrel, but you wouldn't find six bits in the bottom when you'd done it."

If that was true, it was right peculiar, Loco thought. If the settlers were marketing the rustled beef, they should be turning enough profit to spend a little. And they *had* to have money if they were hiring Ray deVaca. Ray might have the heart of an *insurrecto*, but he had the soul of a filibuster. He'd fight for a cause all right, but only when there was the prospect of a profit in it. Maybe every cent the settlers could scrape up was going into that fund. But still, it didn't quite make sense. Why go to all the trouble of swiping someone else's stock and selling it, just to raise enough money to hire a gunman to protect yourself from the people you were stealing from? Especially when you'd end up driving them out of business and cut yourself off from more stock to steal.

Well, somebody must have it all figured out to show himself a pocketful of cash, or there wouldn't be any rustling in the first place.

He nudged the empty cup toward the storekeeper.

"You wouldn't want to fill this up again, would you?"

"Hell, no!"

Shrugging, he turned and threaded his way through the heaps of merchandise to look out the grimy window in the direction he'd come from. The wagon track was empty. He scanned the land around it and decided on a likely patch of scrub on the peak of a rise.

"I'll be back," he said, stepping toward the door into the cabin.

"Hey, you can't . . ." the storekeeper shouted at him as he shoved aside the blanket. He went through the cabin. As he'd expected, there was a back door. He slipped out, keeping close to the wall.

Working his way to the corner of the building, he turned. He kept the building between himself and that patch of brush in the distance as he sauntered down the slope. It was a long walk, especially on a sore foot. He hoped it'd be worth the trouble. Staying in the hollows and gullies, he trekked back toward the brush.

Eventually, he sighted a horse. It stood groundhitched a ways behind the rise that the brush topped. As he approached, it gave him a curious glance, then went on nibbling at the grass. He moved in a little closer, studying the brush. There were boots planted among the roots of the stuff. Branches and new-sprung leaves were almost enough to hide the figure of a man hunkered there.

Loco wondered just how intent he was on the store and the dun still tied at the rail. How alert was he to whatever might happen back here behind him? One way to find out.

Stepping back, Loco ducked behind a thrust of rock that would hide him. He scooped up a handful of gravel. But just as he started to fling it, he heard a strange noise. Motionless, he waited and listened.

There was a faint stirring of branches, then a sharp scrape. He frowned as he tried to place the sound. Then he grinned, almost in disbelief. The gentle breeze brought him a whiff of sulphur. He chanced poking his head up

enough to take a look. Sure enough, a thin wisp of smoke
rose from the bushes. The man hiding there had decided
to have himself a cigarette.

Nearly laughing, Loco revised his plans. He tossed the
gravel. The horse jerked its head up, questioning the
slight sound with its ears, but there was no reaction at all
from the brush. Whoever was hid there was a complete
fool, Loco thought. He wondered which one of them it
was.

The horse paid him a little attention as he strolled out
of hiding. But it didn't seem very interested until he lifted
the nigh stirrup. The saddle was a tie-hard rimfire studded
all the way around with brass nailheads. They'd been
driven into almost every bit of leather possible. He
dropped one cinch, then loosed the other. The horse sighed
like a woman stepping out of her stays.

He let the second cinch down cautiously. He didn't
want the dangling iron rings to clink against each other.
The horse gave him a friendly nudge as he walked around
to gather up the cinch rings. He tied them to a saddle
string, then quietly slid the saddle and its blanket from
the animal's back onto his shoulder. Grinning to himself,
he glanced toward the brush. Smoke still threaded up from
it. He hoped the fool was enjoying that quirly.

As he started away, the horse considered following him.
It took a tentative step and put a forehoof on one rein,
jerking the bit. It paused to give the problem a lot more
thought. Finally it went back to nibbling at the grass.

Loco didn't whistle out loud, but a piece of a tune was
running happily through his head as he sauntered back the
way he'd come. The saddle was heavy, and the walk a long
one. He was limping, but he was still grinning when he got
to the store again. The trip had been worth the trouble.

He approached from the off side of the building, keeping it between himself and the man in the brush again.
When he shoved through the cabin door, the shopkeeper
jumped up out of a rocker, grabbing a stick of firewood
for a club.

"Hold it," Loco called to him. Stepping inside, he dumped the hefty roping kack on the floor.

Cullough frowned at it curiously. "What's that?"

"Saddle."

"I know it's a saddle, but what for?"

"To set a horse on," Loco grunted, hunkering beside it.

The storekeeper didn't bother to ask any more. Muttering under his breath, he watched Loco open one of the brass-studded saddle pockets and bring out a brown paper-wrapped packet.

Fingering it open, Loco found a handful of hard sugar candies. He held it up toward Cullough. "Have one."

"Don't mind if I do."

Taking a piece for himself, he replaced the package and looked into the other pocket. He grinned again as he pulled out a nigh-new cotton bandana. It looked like it might only have been worn once. He knew when and where. And now he knew who was hiding in the bushes spying on him. He shook out the scarf and held it up to the storekeeper. "This worth two bits?"

Cullough shook his head. "It's been used."

"Not much. You just fold it neat and press it flat under something heavy and nobody'll know the difference."

Cullough took it and studied over it, but he said, "No, not two bits."

Under the bandana, Loco had found a little book with stiff paper covers. He was gazing at the picture on the front, wondering what the story inside might be like. From the look of that picture, it would be right exciting. With a bit of a sigh, he held it toward the storekeeper. "How about this?"

Cullough took it and thumbed through it. "The book *and* the bandana."

"Together they ought to be worth *four* bits," Loco said.

"Unh ugh. Says right here on the cover the book only cost ten cents new."

He looked where the storekeeper's finger pointed. "The book and the bandana to pay what I owe you, and you start a tally for me with another drink."

"The hell! I don't even know you. You don't even work around here. Said so yourself."

"You know I pay my debts." He grinned at Cullough. "Ain't I right this minute paying you for the drink I already cadged?"

"Try paying for the next one in advance."

"S'pose I throw in the rest of the candy?"

"No!" the storekeeper said firmly. But then he shook his head and returned Loco's grin. "All right. A short one."

Loco followed him back into the store. As he set up the drink, Loco scanned the merchandise. Tentatively he said, "There's some gear I sure could use."

"Your credit ain't good for gear," Cullough answered him.

He shrugged, then swallowed down the whiskey. The bargain he'd made satisfied him, and he'd decided he liked this hard-put shopkeeper. He'd settle for what he'd got already. Leaning on the counter, he asked for a few directions. Cullough gave them, no charge.

The Three-Slash-C sounded easy enough to find. But the Sheep seemed to have hidden their settlement as far back from the road and neighboring ranches as they could get it. Too far to reach by nightfall, from the sound of it. Shouldering the saddle, he said, "You won't forget me when my friend shows up asking about me?"

"I won't forget you when I'm in my grave," Cullough muttered gruffly, but there was a trace of amusement in his glinty eyes. "How'll I know this friend of yours?"

"He'll ask for me."

"By name?"

"No. But you'll know him."

"If you say so." The storekeeper shrugged.

Whistling, Loco sauntered out to the dun and dropped the saddle on its back. He cinched up, stepped on board, and took off in the direction he'd come from.

When he reached the brushy crest, he was a little disappointed to find that no one was hiding there now. And

the horse that had been groundhitched in the hollow was
gone. Evidently the kid had given up. He wondered just
how Ronny would explain losing his saddle to the rest of
the roundup crew.

The storekeeper's directions had been pretty good. He
didn't have any trouble locating the Three-Slash-C head-
quarters. The house was a two-story, white clapboard
one with green shutters. The front gallery was trimmed
with steamboat fancywork that must have been hauled in
a long ways. It looked an uncommon fine house for this
high country.

Outbuildings were clustered off a ways from the house.
They were stout, fair-looking buildings too. All painted
and well-kept. With the ranch hands out on the cow
hunt, they had an empty look about them, though. And
only a couple of horses stood in the corral. The bay buffalo pony wasn't one of them.

As he shouted in front of the house, he was aware of
something moving within the shadowed doorway of the
barn. No one showed himself there though. Instead, the
front door of the house opened. A woman stepped out
onto the gallery.

She had to be Ruth's mother, to judge from the likeness
in their faces. This woman would be strong-willed, but
quick to laugh, too. She smiled slightly now as she nodded to him and said, "Evening."

"Evening, Miz Caisson," he replied. He kept his eyes on
her, but he was aware of the figure hulking in the doorway
of the barn and of the muzzle of a long gun pointed in
his direction.

The woman looked at his mount. "Is there something
wrong at the cow camp?"

She'd made a natural-enough assumption. The dun carried the Three-Slash-C on its rump. He wondered whether
he should let her go on thinking he worked for her. As he
considered, he said, "No, ma'am. Not when I left."

Relief brightened her face. "You have a message from
Ruth?"

"No, ma'am." He decided to try the truth. "I'm not a hired hand. But I've come over here from the camp and I was hoping maybe I could bed here tonight. Maybe you got chores need doing I could trade off for a meal?"

Her smile disappeared. There was wariness in her voice. "That horse . . . ?"

"I come by him honest. I got a bill of sale." At least he hoped it was a bill of sale. But he wouldn't have put it past that gray-eyed girl to try some kind of ornery trick on him.

Mrs. Caisson waited expectantly, so he fingered the paper from his pocket and held it out. She stepped to the edge of the gallery to take it. Thumbing it open, she frowned at it.

"Is something wrong?" he asked.

She eyed him narrowly. "What could be wrong?"

It *had* been a trick, he thought darkly. It wouldn't be so bad but that somebody had a gun aimed at him. He wondered just what the paper said and how he could bluff his way out of it. He tried his best, most friendly and innocent smile on the woman.

She didn't smile back. Instead, she looked past him.

Glancing over his shoulder, he saw a rider coming toward the ranch at a gallop. The horse was a bay. The girl on its back was Ruth Caisson.

He sighed, wondering if it were a shotgun or a rifle that was aimed toward him. His spine itched.

CHAPTER 6

"What the devil are you doing here?" Ruth snapped at him as she drew rein. She seemed as much bewildered as angry.

Resting his hands on the saddle horn, Loco gave her a blankly innocent look. "I was hoping I could find a place to bed, maybe eat here."

"Of all the gall!"

Mrs. Caisson held the paper toward her. "Did you give him this, Ruth?"

She nodded. Her mother turned to Loco then and handed it back to him. He glanced at the scrawls on it, wondering just what they meant. As he folded it to stuff it into his pocket again, the woman gave him a smile.

"It doesn't really look like Ruth's writing," she said a little apologetically. "And I didn't think she'd sell that particular horse. It's one of our best."

"Yes'm," he mumbled. Maybe the paper really was a bill of sale after all. Eying Ruth sideways, he hoped she'd say something he could find some meaning in.

She said, "That's not the saddle you had before."

"No, ma'am." He had a feeling she recognized it so he added, "Next time you want a man trailed, send a *man* to do the job."

"What?" she seemed honestly puzzled.

"Wasn't it you who set that kid on my tail?" he asked.

"Ronny? He followed . . . ?" A sudden thought flashed anger into her eyes. "What did you do to Ronny?"

"Nothing."

"Then what are you doing with his saddle?" she demanded.

"Learning him a bit about sneaking around after people. I could have put a bullet into him easier than I got his kack. If it wasn't you sent him after me, who did?"

"You'd better tell me exactly what you're talking about," she said coldly. "And no tricks, mister. There's a gun pointing at you right now."

"I know. Look, why don't we stand down, get comfortable?" He glanced toward Mrs. Caisson. "Maybe you got coffee made?"

"What's this all about?" the woman asked her daughter.

"He's crazy. And a little dangerous."

"Only when I *have* to be." He tried grinning again, but it didn't do any good. The girl's face stayed as stern as granite.

"What about Ronny?" she insisted.

"All right." Shifting in the saddle, he set in to telling her just exactly what had happened. When he'd done, she was gazing at him in slightly incredulous amazement. She shook her head.

Her mother laughed. It was a warm friendly sound. "You *are* crazy."

"Yes'm." He gave her a kind of shy smile.

Ruth obviously didn't want to give in. But a grin tugged at the corners of her mouth. After a moment, she let it have its way.

"That was cruel," she said, sympathy for the boy in her voice. But she was amused as well. "I think he'd have preferred to be shot."

Loco nodded. A kid like that would have a lot of stiff-necked pride. He said, "He can get over a red face. But bullets can get kinda permanent sometimes. Who you s'pose sent him following me?"

"It may have been his own idea," she suggested. "He doesn't exactly feel friendly toward you."

Well, that was to be expected. He assumed a look of hurt innocence. "Sure not many folks around these parts seem very friendly. Don't even ask a man down off his horse when he calls."

He thought he saw a trace of embarrassment in her face. She stopped smiling. "What do you expect? You're a thief and a liar."

"I'm not a liar."

"Do you deny being a thief?"

"No, ma'am. I told you I'm not a liar."

"I'd like to know what this is all about," Mrs. Caisson put in.

"Why don't we all set to some coffee? Maybe you got some cold biscuits and a little preserves or something to go with it?" Loco said. "We could talk about it all."

Ruth gave an exasperated grunt.

Glancing toward the barn, he added, "Maybe that feller'd like to join us. I expect he's getting tired of holding that gun."

"Why not?" Mrs. Caisson lifted an eyebrow at her daughter. "I'm getting tired of standing out here myself. And I do have work in the kitchen."

"I don't trust him," the girl said. "I can't make sense of him."

"I couldn't make sense of your father a lot of the time. That was part of his charm." Smiling, the woman turned to Loco. "Step down and come on inside, young man. You said you wanted to earn a meal. You can do it by explaining yourself to my satisfaction. And my daughter's."

"That may be more of a job than I can handle," he muttered as he slid out of the saddle.

Looking toward the barn, Mrs. Caisson called, "Come on over, Kev. And bring the shotgun."

"Shotgun ain't the thing," Loco said. "You want him armed against me, have him fetch a rifle or a revolver. Shot spreads too much. Could hurt you or your daughter."

Mrs. Caisson eyed him curiously. "That's so."

"Doesn't really matter right now," he told her. "Unless you try some trick on me, you're not going to have any trouble from me. But you might keep it in mind, next time you want to cover some stranger who comes to your door."

He stepped around the bay to offer Ruth a hand. Ignor-

ing him, she gathered her skirts and dismounted without
help. He didn't much blame her for being mad at him. He
just wished she'd get over it.

The man who came from the barn was lean and twisted.
His right shoulder hunched forward and he limped badly.
His face was as pebbly wrinkled as old buckskin and his
beard stubble had a mousy color that could have been
graying or natural-born. At first, he seemed weary with
age. But then Loco looked at his eyes. There was a crisp
vitality in them. This wasn't an *old* man, but one who was
worn out from hard times. Crippled up by some accident
like maybe a bronc. Probably as ornery as a nest of hor-
nets.

Holding the shotgun with its butt under his arm and
the muzzle pointed toward Loco's waist, he asked, "You
want him killed or just run off?"

"I don't think either will be necessary," Mrs. Caisson
answered.

Ruth held out a hand. "Give me the Greener, Kev. You
take care of Sundance."

Reluctantly he handed her the gun and took the reins.
Darting a hard look at Loco, he growled, "This one's no
cowhand."

"I know," the girl said.

"Wouldn't give him no job here. Wouldn't give him
the time of day. You want the dun tended too?"

"Yes, please." She nodded, then turned her back to Loco
and strode on into the house.

Mrs. Caisson smiled at him and gestured for him to
follow.

He hadn't been in houses like this very often. There
was soft carpeting underfoot in the hallway, and pictures
of stern-faced men and gently smiling women looked down
at him from the papered walls. A hat tree in a corner
wore a couple of Stetsons. Ruth paused to add hers.

The kitchen was attached to the back of the house,
northern style. And it was a fancy one, dominated by a
big, black iron range with curly vines and rosebuds cast

onto its panels. Isinglass windows showed the fire busy inside it. The pot simmering on top steamed out a scent of beef stew that stirred his juices. He paused to take a deep breath as he glanced around.

The worktable stretching along one wall had a top of thick planks for most of its length, but there was a stone slab set into one end. A lump of dough sat waiting on the stone, with a rolling pin already flour-dusted beside it.

A separate eating table had side chairs neatly tucked in around it. A checkered tablecloth covered it, and places were set for three. The spooner, cruets, and salt cellar in the middle were kept company by a small vase of flowers. And there was likely a fancy dining room as well.

But the most impressive thing about the kitchen was the copper-lined sink with a pump built right into it. That would sure beat lugging water from a well or a spring. Curious, Loco asked, "You got servants?"

Mrs. Caisson shook her head. "Always preferred tending my own chickens. And John, my husband, liked *my* cooking."

He was mildly surprised. People who could afford it generally wanted to be waited on.

She gestured for him to take a seat at the eating table. He pulled out a chair and settled himself, stretching out his legs and wishing he had the makings. But then some folks said it wasn't proper to smoke around women anyway.

These were unusual women, though, he thought. He'd have understood them better if they'd been living in some log shack or 'dobe, hauling water in buckets and cooking on open fires. He didn't expect women in a fine fancy house like this to be strong and self-reliant, to let the sun shine directly onto their faces, and to smile with such forthright honesty. They didn't fit the patterns for people that he had in his head. More intrigued than ever, he looked toward Ruth.

She'd leaned the shotgun in a corner. She washed her

hands under the pump, then asked her mother, "Anything I can do to help?"

"Get out the cups," Mrs. Caisson said, looking into a coffeepot. She reached down a tin of beans and began to feed them into a grinder.

"I can do that for you," Loco offered, starting to his feet.

"No, you relax. And start talking. You've got me as curious as a white-tail doe."

Ruth looked toward him with a trace of apprehension. Her gray eyes were very serious.

She was afraid he'd say something she didn't want her mother to hear, he decided. He began, "Ain't much to tell. I just come drifting up from Mexico, and your people mistook me for somebody else. I spent the night at your roundup camp and kinda got into a fight there. I don't think I exactly convinced everybody I wasn't who they'd mistook me for. I s'pose that's why the kid was following me."

"That's hardly the whole of it," Mrs. Caisson said "Who'd you fight with?"

"Your coosie."

"Can't say I'm surprised." She turned her attention to her daughter. "Who did you mistake him for?"

"The man we'd heard the Sheep had sent for," Ruth told her.

She nodded as if she knew the rumors and the trouble that was brewing. Looking to Loco again, she asked, *"Are* you?"

"No, ma'am."

"But you didn't just *happen* by this particular ranch tonight? You came here intentionally?"

"Yes'm," he allowed.

"Why?" Ruth demanded.

"Figured your ma might be as good a cook as your coosie."

Mrs. Caisson smiled at him. "I hope you aren't planning to fight me, too."

He grinned, liking this woman. "No, ma'am, I sure wouldn't want to square off against *you*."

Impatience overwhelmed Ruth. She faced her mother. "Don't you know what this man is?"

"I know he's rather charming and completely devious."

"I'm *what?*" he said, blank-faced.

"Devious!" Ruth glowered at him. "And don't tell me you don't know what it means."

He shrugged.

"You know a lot more than you're willing to admit," she accused.

"I know mostly what a man learns in a life of drifting," he answered with a deprecating gesture. "I know a lot about some things and not much about others."

Mrs. Caisson said, "You know you're *not* explaining yourself to my satisfaction."

He nodded. Sniffing at the aroma of beef stew, he sighed. "I s'pose if I want to eat I'd better get at it."

She smiled in reply. But her daughter wasn't looking at all friendly. The girl demanded, "What is it you want here?"

"A meal. A place to bed the night."

Color was rising in her face. The gray eyes were flint, striking sparks. He could almost hear her fuse sputtering.

Mrs. Caisson's patience was beginning to wear a bit, too. She asked, "Does it really serve your purpose to be so devious?"

"Maybe not," he owned. "But it's kinda fun."

"Of all the . . . !" Ruth hesitated. She couldn't find a word adequate to express herself.

"All right," Loco said, putting his mind to the job at hand. "I'm curious by nature. Fact is, I'm nosy as hell. I got dragged into the trouble that's brewing around here, and now I fancy finding out just exactly what's going on between you ranchers and the settlers."

The coffeepot had begun to make happy noises. Mrs. Caisson wrapped a pot holder around the handle and brought it to the table. As she tilted it over Loco's cup, she lifted an eyebrow at him. *"And . . . ?"*

He wondered what made her so sure there was more to it than he'd said. He decided she was just plain clever.

The table sweetening was sugar. He spooned some into the coffee and stirred it as he considered. The women watched him silently but insistently. Finally he told them, "You people are all bent on getting yourselves into a fight with these nesters you call Sheep. If your hired hands are as good at fighting them as they were at hauling me down, and if the Sheep really are bringing in professional help, then you're in bad trouble."

"We can take care of ourselves," Ruth said stonily.

"Can you?"

She nodded. But her mother asked, "You think *we* need professional help, too?"

"You're sure gonna need some kind of help if you want to survive."

The girl snapped sarcastically, "Are you offering your services?"

"I'm thinking on it," he muttered. He sipped at the coffee. It was almost as hot as Ruth's anger. It burnt his tongue.

Drawing a deep breath, the girl steadied herself. She looked as if she'd like to level a gun at him again, maybe this time pull the trigger. With as much contempt and scorn as she could, she said, "Just what would you consider your services to be worth?"

"Oh, say, five thousand. In gold."

"Of all the . . . !" You think you're pretty good, don't you?"

"If I weren't good at what I do, I wouldn't be alive," he told her.

Mrs. Caisson looked curious and serious, and still a bit amused. She asked, "Exactly what is it that you do?"

"Pretty much whatever I please to."

"What do you usually please to do?" Ruth growled. "What qualifications do you think you have to ask a price like five thousand dollars for your services?"

For an instant he grinned. Then he blanked his face and answered blandly, "Lately, I've been gunrunning."

She looked shocked. And a little horrified.

Her mother had sense enough to ask, "Where? For whom?"

"Into Mexico. For peons."

"Insurrectionists?"

He nodded.

With a touch of bewilderment, Ruth mumbled, "I thought—*Indians*."

"I know what you thought. You can jump higher and wider to conclusions than anybody I ever met before."

"I'm not sure I approve of revolution," Mrs. Caisson said thoughtfully.

"Maybe *you* never needed one." He glanced significantly around the fancy kitchen, then settled his gaze on the girl. "And there were Indians among them. *Indios, Mestizos, Criollos—people*—just plain people who . . . maybe you never seen scrawny, bowlegged kids digging in garbage heaps for scraps to eat on. . . ." He stopped himself, aware that he was losing hold of his own temper. He didn't want to start fighting that war with these people.

Mrs. Caisson was peering at him in a curious way that made him uncomfortable. He rubbed his fingertips at the scar over his right eye, not aware that he was doing it, and grunted. "All right, I'm a thief and a filibuster, and maybe that's what you need around here."

"I'm not sure what we need," the woman said. She had already poured coffee for herself and her daughter. Turning, she set the pot on the stove. With her back to Loco, she went on, "In any case, we couldn't afford anything like five thousand dollars for help. The way things are now, we're drowning in debts."

"I'm not asking anything like five thousand dollars," he said.

She faced him again, frowning in question. And Ruth started, "But you said . . ."

"I said I'm *worth* it," he interrupted. "I'm not *asking* it."

"What are you asking?" Mrs. Caisson put in.

"Right now I'm broke. I need coin and found. *If* I decide I want to work for you, I'll do it for a cowhand's wage."

"If?"

Ruth snapped, "Suppose we don't *want* you working for us?"

He shrugged.

Mrs. Caisson was eying him in speculation. But she spoke to the girl. "Suppose you set another place at the table. We'll eat first and finish our talking later. Maybe in the morning when everyone's had a chance to rest and do some thinking."

With a sigh of disgust, Ruth wheeled away. She jerked open a door of the china cupboard. Taking out a plate, she slapped it down on the table, then went to fetch the silver.

Her eyes still smoldered with anger, but Loco had a notion she was glad to postpone the talk too. She had sense enough to know he was right, but at the moment she was too mad to admit it.

He told himself he had to stop prodding her in the pride. Even if it was fun, it was hardly the way to win her over as a friend. Grinning slightly, he owned to himself that what he wanted here was something more than just friendship.

Mrs. Caisson was cutting biscuits from the dough she'd rolled. Leaning back in the chair, he sipped his coffee and watched her. The warm scents of the simmering stew and the fresh-made coffee surrounded him. A few minutes after she put the first pan of biscuits into the oven, they were adding their aroma. It was pleasant. Real pleasant.

What would it be like to live in a house of this kind, he wondered. What would it be like to own land and cattle and coin? To have a kitchen like this, and a bed—and a wife to keep them both warm?

Likely *real* pleasant.

CHAPTER 7

The food was good, but the meal was silent and strained. The ranch hand Kev didn't help the mood any at all. He acted as surly toward Loco as ever Ruth had, though he lacked her reasons. Loco figured it was just the man's nature. Anyone lamed up that bad had a right to be sour.

When they'd done eating, Mrs. Caisson told Kev to show Loco to the bunkhouse, explaining that he'd sleep there the night. Loco halfway expected the ranch hand to have some objection, but Kev just glowered and gestured for him to follow. Outside, he matched the man's pace. For a lame, shuffling gait, it covered ground fast enough.

They had almost reached the dark looming hulk of the bunkhouse when Kev stopped suddenly. "I ain't too spry," he grumbled. "But you look limber enough. Step back to the house and fetch some matches, will you?"

"Sure." Loco strode back and knocked at the door. Mrs. Caisson answered it. She seemed surprised when he asked for matches, but she dug up a tin boxful and gave them to him.

When he got back to the bunkhouse, Kev was standing by the open door. He gestured Loco inside.

Usually there'd be a lantern hanging just inside a door-jamb. Loco stepped into the darkness, reaching out to feel for one.

Dull red sparks of pain exploded suddenly inside his skull as something slammed hard against the back of his head. He felt himself stumbling. His shoulder hit something hard. A post. An upright supporting one of the bunks. He felt the corner of the wood pressing against his cheek. For a moment he leaned against it, trying to

cling to it. His arm wrapped around it, but there was no
strength in his grip. His knees were buckling, his hand
sliding on the post. He was folding up like a sack with
the grain spilling out.

His thoughts were shredding into thin, ragged fragments.
He had an awareness that he'd been buffaloed, a knowledge that he was still falling, a vague impression that
there was more than one man in the darkness around him.

His knees hit the floor first. He felt the jar clear up
through his skull. His outstretched hands struck and the
arms crumpled under him. Sprawling face down on the
floor, he lay motionless. Unable to move. For an instant,
he felt panic. Then nothing.

It was an old darkness, and old memories stirred
through it like wisps of fog rising off the river at night.
The boy huddled, shivering, hearing the faraway call of
a boat moving through darkness. The wind off the water
was cold. It had the teeth of coming winter, and he
thought he wanted to leave this place. This was a no-good
town. Even the rats were gaunt and eternally hungry here.
Too few rags or bones or old bottles, too many people
hunting scraps they could sell—or eat. A no-good town.
The sounds of water lapped at the pilings of the old pier.
The wood creaked. Something scurried along close by.
He knew that tapping of four small clawed feet and a hard
hairless tail. The sound was as cold as the wind. God, how
he hated the rats. . . .

The smell was of an animal. Not a rat though. A warm,
familiar scent close against his face. The sweaty hide of
a horse. He recalled a horse. He'd been maybe half-grown
then, when he'd stolen the horse from the knacker. An
ancient bonerack with mournfully sad eyes. He'd thought
it must know why it was at that place, and he'd wanted
to help it get away. To help himself get away, too.

A poor old condemned horse with white splotches
of collar scars on its neck and whip welts on its rump,
and a way of nuzzling at his ear, breathing warmly down

his neck. A castoff, windbroken animal, but it had carried him a long way before it finally lay down one day in a daisy-yellow field and died with its head in his lap.

Vaguely he realized it had been a long time ago that he'd stolen the horse from the knacker and headed west, leaving behind the river with its stink of dead fish and the cities with their cold stone streets and stench of rotting garbage. This was some other horse, some other time.

He realized that he was bellied down across the animal's back. His head hung too low, and it was filled with pain. Each jarring step the horse took hammered inside his skull. He tried to move. That was when he found he was tied. And he understood he was in trouble.

New memories, sharp-edged as razors, cut into the mists in his mind. He remembered he'd been bushwhacked. By the ranch hand Kev, he thought. At Ruth Caisson's order?

He didn't think they planned to kill him. If they'd simply wanted him dead, they'd have finished the job already. Someone was leading the horse that carried him. Taking him off somewhere. Not to jail, he hoped. He could stand damned near anything—except being locked up. They kept trying to lock him up. All his life, they'd kept trying it. And he'd kept running. . . .

The horse stopped.

He was still badly dazed when they dragged him down from its back. They let him drop to the ground. He lay limp, aware that there was no use trying to move. His hands were tied in front of him, and his body felt as weak as if his bones were all crumbled. The pain in his head kept throbbing like a smith's hammer pounding his thoughts to pieces.

He thought there were only two or three of them, but in the night-dark it was hard to be sure. His eyes wouldn't accept the shadowy figures as more than blurs. They seemed to have their faces covered with scarfs, and they spoke tersely in hoarse grunts. They dragged him to his feet, leaning his back against the trunk of a tree. One held him there while another threaded a length of rope around

his arms. Around the tree, too. When they pulled it taut,
it jerked back his elbows, straining at the thong holding his
wrists. He was lashed tight against the tree trunk. To be
shot, or abandoned, or what?

Forcing unwilling neck muscles, he lifted his head and
tried to see them. Dark figures barely given shape by the
dim moonlight. One coming close, cursing softly under
the muffling kerchief over his mouth.

The fist hit like the kick of a mule against Loco's gut.
He flinched, grunting at the driving pain. The thongs cut
deep into his wrists. The fist hit him again.

He let his head lob forward. The fist rose, knuckles
ramming into his face, jolting his head back. It hit the
tree. The back of his skull was already sore. The blow
struck both ways, shooting new pain through his face,
spattering fresh sparks of it inside his head.

The one who was beating him did it with a wild aban-
don, a cursing excited pleasure. The flailing fists hammered at his belly. The pain spread through him until it
became his entire being. He knew nothing else. It overwhelmed him, smothering him.

The darkness was a rat as big as the world. At first it
nibbled and gnawed. Then it swallowed him whole.

"Hey, crazy man, you going to wake up or die? Make
up your mind, huh?"

The words were tiny bursts of flame inside his skull. His
head was stuffed with pain. There was no room for the
sounds. They jabbed, squeezing and searing.

"Shut up!" he thought.

"Wake up, you damned *gringo chiflado*," the little
flames demanded.

Centipedes were walking over his face. Wearing boots.
Dragging their spurs. Cold, sharp, prickly, trickling little
feet. Vaguely he realized that a wet cloth was being wiped
across his forehead. He recognized the voice that was trying to call him out of darkness. He thought he wanted to
open his eyes.

Pale light and grayish blurs. A shape he couldn't make into a face, though he knew it must be one. Pieces of memory.

"I lost another horse," he thought. He heard a grumbling like a far-off landslide within his head and he knew he'd said it out loud.

The voice of Ray deVaca laughed and cursed and then said, "Hey, Loco, you got somebody mad at you or something?"

"Amigos," he mumbled, knowing that this time he was saying it as well as thinking it. He had an awareness of his mouth, swollen and painful. The words dragged off a thick tongue. *"Todos amigos. Siempre."*

"Talk English, you lousy chino. You got Spanish like a jackass."

"Got Spanish like *piojos*. Catch it off my friends." Talking hurt. Everything hurt. But the pain had a crisp sharpness that assured him he was alive. Ignore it and it'll go away, he told himself. Squinting, he tried again to make the blur become a face. It still refused.

Something touched his neck. It slid under his head and shoved. The mushy ooze his brains had become sloshed inside his skull as his head was lifted, tilted forward. The world spun around him.

"Whoa, leggo," he groaned. Something touched his lips. Hard. Cool. Then wet. DeVaca trickled the water carefully into his mouth, but even so he almost choked on it. His throat didn't want to work. When it finally swallowed, the water felt like lumps of scrap iron going down his gullet.

A voice that wasn't deVaca's asked, "How is he?"

"How is rawhide? You want to hurt it, you got to put holes in it. Him, too."

"I hurt," Loco mumbled.

DeVaca jostled his head, pouring more water into his mouth. And then something that wasn't water. Liquid fire? Acid? Corn singlings? Something that peeled the skin off his tongue. He tried to lift a hand, groping for water to splash on the flames. He couldn't tell whether the hand moved or not. But deVaca gave him more water.

The fire sunk down to embers. A little lump of numbness began in his belly. It was growing, spreading through him, stifling the pain.

"Wha's that?" he managed to ask.

"Laudanum. You'll feel better soon. Sleep, huh?"

He felt his head being lowered. It sunk deep into something soft. The whole of him was sinking. Pain was fading into a far distance. He floated in misty clouds. The tender, heavy eyelids wanted to close. Not yet, he thought, fighting them.

"Who?" DeVaca was asking. "Ranchers?"

"Yeah."

"You want me to kill a couple for you, huh?"

"No." He wasn't sure why. Not sure of anything. Didn't want Ray killing anyone. Had to understand first. Couldn't think straight. He repeated it faintly, "No."

"Ah? When you are better? You want to see it, to do it yourself, huh? *Bueno.* We'll wait."

"Lost my horse again," he thought dimly. He must have said it. He heard Ray answering him.

"Always the horses, eh, *charro*? A man is no man without a horse, huh? You sleep some more. When you are ready to ride, you'll have a horse. I promise you that."

It was dark. A soft enveloping darkness. Ray's words trailed thinly into it. He wanted to say something more to Ray. But he had only a vague awareness of his body. He wasn't sure whether he was speaking aloud or not. "Don' go 'way, *'mano.*"

"I'll be here," Ray assured him. His voice was soft and concerned. It sounded far distant, as lone and lost as the first evening star. "You just make sure you do wake up again, *amigo mio.*"

Loco woke. He lay in arnica-scented silence with his eyes closed, remembering. He'd been beaten. He'd been in a long deep unconsciousness and in dream-ridden sleep.

He had been awake after a fashion a few times already. There were faint recollections of Ray deVaca at his side, feeding him thick gruel from a spoon and cursing him affectionately.

But he'd been sick and numbed with laudanum then, and those memories were hazy. Now he was really awake. His curiosity stirred itself and urged him to open his eyes.

There was dim light. It seemed to flow from a white square above him. Squinting, he focused on a piece of sacking that covered a window. It fluttered like the window was open, but he couldn't catch the odors of the air. The smell of arnica was too strong.

He was lying on a feather-bed pallet, with a pillow under his head and a quilt over his body. Turning his head slightly, he wondered where he was.

He'd been dimly aware before that he was in a room. Now it had shape for him. An empty room with a hard-packed earth floor, chinked pole walls, low beams overhead with shadowed emptiness above them. Another covered window in the far wall. A batten door. Closed. But not locked, he hoped.

Likely this was an outbuilding, he thought. There was no fireplace or stove or smoke hole. No furniture except a spindly table, a lone chair, and another pallet like the one he lay on. A lantern and several bottles sat on the table. Not whiskey bottles, though. Probaby laudanum and arnica.

Close to his bed were a couple of buckets. The handle of a dipper stuck up out of one. He wanted the other one. And he wanted to know if he had the strength to tend himself.

His chest and his belly hurt. His wrists were sore and his hands felt numb. His arms and legs seemed watery weak. It took determination to get himself sitting up. Determination edged with a fear of helplessness drove him the rest of the way onto his feet.

He had to lean against the wall—to hang onto it—or the world that was high-rolling and sunfishing under him

might fling him off. He'd been thrown before. Once dragged
a ways by a stirrup before he'd managed to get hold of
his revolver and put enough slugs into the runaway to stop
it. He'd felt something like this then. Not quite so bad
though. He hung onto the wall, and after a while the world
eased its pitching.

He'd never worn a nightshirt before. It struck him as a
useless thing. Too drafty to keep a man warm in the
winter. Too much trouble if the weather turned hot. And
no good at all if he had to take to the saddle in a hurry.
He wondered whose it was he had on now. And where
were his own clothes?

Finished with the bucket, he leaned against the wall and
considered. He really wanted to know where he was and
whether or not that door was locked. Could he make it
across the room? Worth trying, he decided.

It was no easy trip. His knees wanted to fold up under
him. Each step he took pulled the aching muscles over his
belly. He clenched his teeth, and the hinges of his jaws
hurt. His brains sloshed and his head spun and even drawing shallow breaths was a painful business. But once he'd
begun the long walk to the door, he was determined to
finish it.

At last he reached the far wall. Staggering, he almost
fell against it. He leaned there, exhausted, hanging on for
long, long moments. When the world had steadied again,
he tried the door. It wasn't locked.

With a sense of relief, he edged it open a crack and
looked out. Narrowing his eyes against the harsh sunlight,
he made out a stretch of yard and the backside of a cabin.
A rough-hewn log wall with a door and a couple of glass-
paned windows. A plank step up to the doorsill. Chickens
puttering around the step. A hog nosing at a clump of
weeds. A speckled hound lying asleep in the sunlight. A
green farm wagon with yellow wheels, dusty and scab-
bing its paint.

The cabin door opened. It was a woman who came out.
Looked youngish. Hard to tell. His eyes didn't want to

sharpen her image for him. She wore something dark. A loose flowing dress that looked almost like a sack with sleeves. White apron over it. Brownish hair, done up in some kind of tight bun.

Carrying a basin, she trod along the puncheons stretched from the back door, off from the cabin a short ways. She flung water from the basin into a puddle. The hog sauntered over and waded in. The girl turned, starting back to the cabin. That was when she saw Loco.

"Hey, mister! Seen-yor . . ." she began, coming toward him. Suddenly she stopped and wheeled. Her back to him, she said hesitantly, "You—you shouldn't be up."

It took him a moment to understand what had shocked her. Grinning, he said, "Sorry, somebody's took my britches."

He could see the redness on the back of her neck. She stood rigid, facing into the distance. Sounding abashed, she stammered, "I—I've been washing them. I never saw leather . . ." She paused, then spoke the word as if it weren't quite fit for proper folk, *"trousers* before."

It struck him funny that a woman might wash a man's britches, but couldn't rightly talk about them. He asked, "What'd you wash 'em with?"

"Harness soap."

That was all right. It wouldn't leech out the life that was left in the old leather, the way lye soap would.

"You shouldn't be up, seen-yor," she repeated. "You were hurt bad. You ought to stay in bed."

"Help me," he suggested.

The blush burned bright red on her neck again. Her face was probably red as a beet, he thought. She was about the shyest girl he'd ever run onto. Her voice came thin, almost weak. "I—I *couldn't!"*

"If I let go this doorpost, I'll fall flat on my face." He had a feeling that might not be a lie.

He caught her sympathy all right. But she told him, "I'll fetch help."

"No! Look, you don't want to leave me hanging on

here while you hunt around for help. Just give me a hand. It'll only take a minute."

"I *couldn't* . . . could I?"

"I need help, ma'am." What the devil was that word? "A Samaritan."

Her head turned slightly. She sneaked a quick look at him over her shoulder. Her face glowed a brilliant red. "I suppose—it would be the *Christian* thing to do."

"Yes'm." He kept the grin off his face.

She turned very slowly toward him. From the look of her, she was going against all the training of a lifetime. She held a hand out at arm's length.

"You got to come closer," he told her.

It took a little coaxing to get her up to his side. Finally, she made it. He slid his arm over her shoulder. At his touch, she flinched. He could feel the tension in her. But she didn't draw away.

"You better put your arm around me," he said.

She wrapped it so lightly around his waist that he could barely feel it. The touch was a faint tickling. He leaned against her, knowing for sure now that he was still alive. Taking a slow step, he muttered, "Easy, ma'am."

She looked sideways into his face. There was a small sparkle in her eyes. She was doing something she figured was terribly daring, and not at all proper, he thought. And she was finding out she enjoyed it. He gave her a smile. "I'm grateful for your help, ma'am."

The color in her cheeks began to ease, but the tension didn't. He could feel it under the arm he rested on her shoulder and where his side pressed against hers. Taut muscles, but with a warm softness even so. He had a notion it might be a right nice body hidden under that sack of a dress.

Gently, very slowly, step-by-step, she walked him across the room to the pallet. Tenderly, she helped him down.

He knew he was alive all right. And too damned hurting to do anything about it. He felt a little disgusted with himself. Sitting with his back against the wall, he grinned at her.

"You look feverish," she said.

"I am."

He had the quilt pulled up to his waist now. That seemed to satisfy her sense of what was proper. The apprehension in her was fading. With concern in her eyes, she pulled a wadded kerchief out of her apron pocket. She dipped it into the water bucket, then bent to touch it gently to his face.

"That help?" she asked.

"Yes'm."

"Is there anything you want?"

He knew better than to answer that. Instead, he decided to coax her into keeping him company awhile, if he could. He said, "Who are you?"

"Esther Shepherd."

CHAPTER 8

Loco sat leaning back against the wall gazing at the girl. Long lashes hid her downcast eyes. He couldn't make out their color, but he knew they were sparkling.

It was a gentle, bashful, lovely face. A warm and lovely young girl. And her name was Esther Shepherd.

Yeah, Shepherd. That was the name the wrangler had mentioned—the bossman of the Sheep. He told himself he should have realized it already. Where the hell did he expect he was with Ray deVaca around?

She was probably close kin to the bossman, he thought. Likely his daughter. He asked *"Miss* Shepherd?"

She nodded.

He didn't quite know how to put his next question. He didn't suppose these people would take very kindly to being called Sheep to their faces. He said, "This place, it's a settlement of religious folk?"

"Yes." There was pride in her voice. "We've come here to found the new Kingdom of the Lord on Earth."

"You're like the Saints?"

"No, we aren't Mormons or Shakers or Quakers or anything like that. We're ourselves."

"What do you call yourselves?"

"We don't have a name. We—what's the matter?"

"Nothing," he mumbled. She'd startled him. But he told himself it wouldn't be the same at all. When a man didn't have a name it was because he didn't know who his folks had been, or where he'd come from, or where he belonged. But these people would all have names and families and homes. Even if they didn't have a label for their religion, they'd know where it came from. And they believed they belonged here.

The girl was smiling at him and saying, "Seenyor de-Vaca called you Loco. Is that your name?"

"It's what I'm called."

"Is it Mexican?"

He nodded.

"You talk American real good," she said.

"*Gracias.*" He grinned at her, warmly amused.

"What's that mean?"

Before he could answer, a man's voice called from the yard, "Essie! Where are you?"

"That's Pa!" She jumped up, swiping at her skirts to smooth them. Scurrying to the door, she dashed out. She left it open behind her.

Loco gazed at it, feeling apprehensive now. Religious folk were generally *very* particular about their girl-children being alone with strange men. What would this Shepherd be like? He'd seen a few hell-fire preachers he'd sooner not tangle with, no matter how fit he was feeling. He sure didn't feel much like a fight right now.

It didn't take long. A man appeared in the doorway, hesitating there for a moment, then striding over to the pallet. He stood looking down at Loco.

He was built short, with heavy bone, and a skin way too big for him. It wrinkled and sagged, hanging in loose waddles from his jaws and neck. It pouched around his mild hazel eyes. Hanks of graying hair tufted above his ears. Wisps of it fuzzed scantily over the top of his round head. His face was shaven clean but not close. The whitish stubble made it look very soft, almost weak.

This had been a jolly fat man not too long ago, Loco thought with surprise. He looked like he'd been bad sick or something. Sure didn't resemble any of the hell-fire preachers Loco had seen ranting on street corners. Didn't look like a leader of men at all. Maybe he wasn't Shepherd, the bossman. . . .

As if answering the unspoken thought, the man said, "I am Silas Shepherd."

The voice was as mild as the eyes, but it had a firm strength underlying it. Studying the face, Loco decided there was strength hidden in it. The first impression of this man was a wrong one.

"My daughter, Essie, was in here with you," Shepherd continued. It was half question, half statement.

"She was helping me," Loco told him.

Stiffly, he hunkered to look straight into Loco's face. He spoke with quiet sincerity. "I want you to understand, boy. This Seenyor deVaca says you're his friend and you come here to help him. Says he can use your help all right. And you were sure needing somebody's help when you got here. We're Christian folk and, whatever you are, we wouldn't turn you away sick and hurt. But you're *not* one of us. You don't *belong* here. You understand that?"

"You don't want me talking to your daughter."

"You got the gist of it."

Loco nodded. He'd got the gist of speeches like that before. Usually they were put into stronger language, though. Sometimes backed with a handful of lead. And no matter how it was put, he didn't like it. Wearily, he said, "I don't see anything wrong with me just *talking* to her."

"All the serpent did was *talk* to Eve."

"What's that supposed to mean?" Loco asked.

"We're gonna build a new Eden here. I figure the Lord had His reasons for letting the serpent into the first Eden and He's got His reasons for putting trials and tribulations on to us now. He guided us in sending for your friend, de-Vaca, and now He's sent you to us. He had his reasons for letting Cain live, too. I won't question His ways. . . ."

That's damned decent of you, Loco thought, *but he kept his mouth shut. The image in front of him blurred. He blinked, trying to hold Shepherd in focus. His head was getting wobbly again. It felt like his strength was running out.*

". . . But I'll tell you, boy," Shepherd went on. "You'll be here just long enough to tend your mission. Then you'll be gone. You'll leave nothing here behind you. You won't go putting notions into my girl's head that she'll keep remembering. If you want a woman to talk to, or anything else, you go off to the land of Nod where you belong."

"Huh?" That didn't make any sense at all to Loco. He'd never heard of a place called Nod. But he didn't feel much like wondering about it now. He wished Shepherd would get done talking and go away.

Rising, the man looked down on him. "We're peaceful people. We're the Lord's folk and we follow His ways. We keep His commandments. But there've been times when He's led His people into wars and killings. If that's how He commands us now, it's what we'll do. You understand me?"

It sounded like a threat. The mild-eyed little man seemed to be saying he was willing to back his hand with lead if he thought it was needed.

"Understand me?" he repeated.

"Mister, I don't understand religious talk at all," Loco mumbled.

"I don't expect you to," Shepherd said with a sigh. "I'm just telling you to stay away from my girl. You understand *that?*"

"Yeah, but . . ."

"If you need help, you get it from your friend. If he ain't around, get it from me. *Not* from my girl." With that the man wheeled and stalked toward the door.

Like hell, Loco thought. *If I'm good enough to fight your damned war, I'm good enough to talk to your daughter. And I'm good enough to put you down, old man. Fists or a knife or a gun, however you want it.*

Not today though, he had to allow to himself. He was still sick with hurting. Too weak to be of much use to himself. Carefully, he eased his head down onto the pillow. Stretching out, he closed his eyes.

Ray deVaca located a galvanized bathtub somewhere around the settlement. He dragged it into the outshed they'd been quartered in, and filled it with water hot enough to scald the hair off a goat hide.

Loco had to have help peeling the nightshirt. Once it was off, he discovered his belly was covered with splotches of bruise the color of rotting plums. It felt like the color might go clear through to his backbone. The hurting sure did.

Dark bands of bruise wrapped around his wrists where the thongs had dug in. His fingers were stiff. A little swollen, he thought.

He eased away the hand that had clung to Ray for support. Balancing carefully on his own feet, he scowled at the surface of the water.

"I should have warned you," Ray was saying. "Should have told you why we were coming up here. Who to look out for. They sure beat you up good, them ranchers."

"Yeah," Loco muttered, prodding himself very gently in the ribs. Even a light touch hurt. He was surprised none of his ribs had been broken. "How'd I get here, Ray? How'd you find me?"

"Didn't find you. Ranchers brought you here. Come riding through in the middle of the night. Three or four of them. Galloped through in the dark. We heard 'em, ran out to see what was happening. Found you in the road. You sure looked dead."

"Maybe they thought I was."

Ray grinned at him. "Not enough though, huh? What you done before I got here? How'd they catch onto you?"

"They were expecting a gunhand from Mexico. Thought I was him—you."

"Oh? So you took this beating for me, *amigo?*"

"No," he mumbled, bending cautiously. None of his belly muscles wanted to flex. And his head felt like it might fall off. He touched a fingertip to the water. It was cooling. Might be bearable, he thought.

"What do you mean, no?"

"No, it wasn't for you. Gimme a hand, huh?"

Ray helped him into the tub. He winced, tensing against the heat. That hurt too. Dammit, everything hurt. How long would it be before he was himself again? He eased his head to rest against the tub's high back and closed his eyes, thinking of Ruth Caisson.

"The beating was meant for *me* all right," he said. Dammit, he'd been honest with those Caisson women. Too honest, he supposed. And he'd even thought they believed him. That had been his mistake—liking Ruth and trusting her. He'd set himself up and let her bear-trap him good on her second try.

He had meant to help her against the Sheep. He'd really *wanted* to. So she'd had him hammered into a purple pulp and dropped off in the settlement. She'd given him to the Sheep. All right, if that was the way she wanted it . . .

"You see 'em?" Ray was asking him. "You know which ones it was?"

"Unh ugh, didn't see 'em. But I guess I know."

"We'll even it up, huh? How's that water?"

"Hotter'n hell." It felt good though. Once it stopped burning, it sucked at the soreness in him. He thought it would be easy to fall asleep lying there. Probably slide in and drown if he did. Damned near drowned once in the river. Trying to haul out a sack of kittens someone had thrown off the wharf. Ended up having to be hauled out himself, by that big zambo who steeved for the Langley people. Hadn't managed to save the kittens, but the zambo had taken him home to that shack in the marsh to dry off. Shared a whopping big fish with him. He smiled slightly at the memory. Wasn't often he'd had his belly as full as that in those days. Poor damned kittens had drowned though.

Why, he wondered dreamily. It was a big world. Hell of a lot of everything in it. Seemed like there ought to be enough for everybody. Why did poor mewling kittens have to be killed, instead of let to live out their lives?

"How you feel?" Ray asked him. "Gonna be good enough to set a horse pretty soon?"

The question pulled him back to wakefulness. He squinted through his lashes. "I reckon. We in a hurry?"

Ray shrugged and smiled. "These people, they're worried. They think soon as the ranchers finish the cow hunt, they'll come make trouble. Want to be ready for it."

"What is it they're expecting us to do?"

The smile became a laugh. "We got to make soldiers out of these *peones.* How you like that?"

"Huh?"

"They think the cowboys are going to attack them. They want to be ready. Know how to fight back. They don't hardly know nothing now, maybe what end of a gun to put the bullets in. That's all. You and me gonna be generals, crazy man. You know what the ranchers call these people? *Sheep.* You and me gonna make soldiers out of *Sheep.*"

"What do you think of 'em?"

"They're good people. And they're gonna pay us good."

"In cattle or money?"

"What cattle? Work ox, milk cow? These people got no cattle. They got money though. . . . " Ray frowned in sudden thought, then grinned. "Hey, sometimes you're pretty smart, Loco. We take the Sheep's money and the ranch cattle, huh?"

"Somebody's already taking the ranch cattle. Where you think these Sheep are getting the money to pay us?"

He shrugged again. "That don't worry me, long as they got it."

Yeah, Loco told himself. Why worry, long as they got the money. Keep your own belly full, *hombre.* Let other people worry about themselves. Let them all drown.

When he'd done bathing, Ray helped him out of the tub and into his clothes. Esther had done a thorough job of washing them. They felt fresh against his scrubbed skin. Despite all the soreness, the sickly weakness, and the dark edges around his thoughts, he decided it was a good day. A day to appreciate being alive. Dressed but for his boots he let go Ray's arm. It wasn't too hard standing alone. He tried a couple of steps and managed it.

"You're all right, huh?" Ray smiled at him.

"I'm hungry." Maybe food would help the feeling of weakness, he thought.

"Enough to eat a horse?"

"Yeah."

Ray's dark eyes shone with some secret thought. "You wait a minute."

Loco watched him hurry off, then walked with careful slowness across the room. He made it without trouble, but it was tiring work. Leaning against the doorjamb, he waited.

Ray came back leading a horse. "A present for you, *amigo*. Want to ride him or eat him?"

Astonished, Loco stared at the dark bay with the slit ears of a buffalo pony, and the Three-Slash-C burned into its rump. *"That* horse? How . . . where . . . ?"

"You like him?" Ray beamed with enthusiasm. "Very good horse, huh? I got him last night, out a rancher's corral. Best horse around, I think. For you, *caballero*."

Loco reached out to stroke the bay's neck. Under its hide, he could feel the fine, hard muscle. It rolled a wary eye, watching him distrustfully, but it didn't flinch away from his touch.

A damned good horse. A very special horse. Of all the animals in this basin, Ray had to choose Ruth Caisson's horse to steal. He muttered, "There's gonna be trouble."

"Yeah." Ray seemed amused by the idea. "Ranchers don't like it, huh? I don't like the way they beat you up, my friend. I thought maybe I keep this horse for myself. But I think the ranchers owe you. So now you got a horse. They owe you a horse, huh?"

Running his hand along the bay's withers, Loco nodded. Ruth Caisson had begun by killing his tobiana. She'd given him the dun, and then taken it back and beaten hell out of him to boot. She damn well owed him a horse, he told himself. And he *wanted* this one. He allowed that he wouldn't have stolen Sundance himself, but now he had the horse here in hand, he sure wasn't willing to give it up easy.

He grinned at Ray. *"Muchas gracias, patrón."*

"Patrón, hell! *Amigo,* crazy man. *Amigo!"*

"Yeah. Only one thing, *amigo.* If I'm gonna keep *this* horse, I'm gonna need a gun. At least, a gun."

"You think they'll try to take him back?"

"I know damn well they will."

Ray laughed. "All right, I'll get you a gun. Maybe a couple."

"And quick."

"You don't need 'em so quick. You ain't ready to ride out and look for trouble yet."

"I don't think I'll have to," Loco answered. "Trouble's likely to ride in looking for me."

Ray's face was suddenly solemn. "I don't like it. You ain't ready for trouble yet."

"Hell, I'm fine," Loco lied. "I can handle anything that comes along."

"Sure." Ray didn't believe him. "Only for now, I'll take the horse, hide him. He'll be waiting when you want him. Right now, you rest some maybe?"

"Yeah, *after* I've ate."

Ray answered him with a flash of a grin and led Sundance away.

He stood watching the smooth action of the bay's stride and the flex of muscle under its shining pelt, until it was gone around a corner of a building. Then he glanced at the marks its hoofs had struck against the hard-packed earth.

How long, he wondered, until trouble tracked that horse here? He hoped Ray'd hurry and scare up a gun for him. He hoped he wouldn't need it too soon. His head was still inclined to start spinning every time he tried to walk more than a couple of steps.

How long?

CHAPTER 9

With his belly full, Loco slept. He was dreaming of trouble when the noises woke him. A slammed door. Someone shouting. The clatter of hoofs, coming in at a gallop, then suddenly stopping.

Was it Ray back from his scout of the countryside with bad news? Or some other kind of trouble arriving? He knew with a certainty that it was trouble. He dragged himself to his feet, still groggy with sleep, and headed out.

At the back corner of Shepherd's cabin, he paused to catch his breath. He had some strength, but not enough. And he didn't have a gun yet. Warily, he made his way to the front of the cabin. There, he stayed to its shadow.

The wheel-rut road ended by swinging in a wide circle and returning on itself. It made a bare-earth plaza of sorts, flanked by cabins. More were scattered within sight. The Sheep seemed to have wanted to stay close together. Maybe they huddled together for protection, he thought.

The rider had drawn rein in the plaza. It was Ruth Caisson. Alone. She sat a snorting, lathered sorrel geld. Her Winchester rested on her bent knee and there was fury in her face.

It looked like a good horse. Good enough for anyone who hadn't owned Sundance. She sat tall on it, with her skirts draping over her legs. Her back was straight and the broad-brimmed hat was square on her head. She held up her chin, gazing down her nose at the man in front of her.

Shepherd stood there with his hat in his hands. Loco couldn't see his face, but his shoulders were set as if he expected a fist fight.

Other men watched Ruth Caisson, too. A half dozen or more of the settlers hung back, close to the cabins, staring. Some had guns in their hands, but none looked prepared to use them.

Leaning against the cabin wall, Loco gazed at the girl with mixed feelings. He admired her nerve, riding into the enemy camp alone like that. But she was a fool to do it. She needed a man with sense to curb her down, he thought. Someone who could appreciate all that fire and handle it without getting hurt.

He savored that thought with wry amusement. He'd got plenty hurt already trying to deal with Ruth Caisson. But he still wanted to try. Hell, don't you know when you're well off, he asked himself. There's more women in the world than one. But not many like Ruth Caisson.

". . . giving you just one warning," she was saying to Shepherd, with a snarling edge to her voice. "I mean to have that horse back, no matter what."

"I don't know anything about your horse," he answered tautly. Not exactly angry and not exactly afraid. Loco couldn't judge just what it was in Shepherd's tone.

"You *can't* think I'm fool enough to believe that," the girl said. Swinging her head, she scanned the settlement as if she expected to see Sundance. "Either I get my horse back now, or I'll ride up to the cow camp and collect some help. I'll come back and *take* him."

"I tell you I don't know anything about your horse," Shepherd insisted. He seemed really hurt that she didn't believe him. "We don't steal. We don't allow thieves among us. We don't . . ."

"Don't you?" she snapped. Her gray eyes were sharp. They'd caught Loco in the shadows, and they held to him.

Taking a step forward, he considered walking up to her. But he didn't want to chance falling flat on his face in front of her. He sidled around the corner of the cabin and leaned his back against the wall.

"Evenin', ma'am," he said, grinning. He hadn't intended to show himself, but he wasn't sorry she'd spotted him. He wanted her to know she hadn't got rid of him with that beating.

She glared at him. *"You've* got Sundance!"

"S'pose I have?"

Wheeling to face him, Shepherd breathed sharply. "Did you steal this woman's horse?"

"No."

The man looked puzzled. But if Ruth had heard the answer, she sure didn't believe it. Her hand was tense on the action of the Winchester. She lifted the muzzle slightly, "I'll kill you."

For an instant, he had the feeling of a man caught in a dream, going through the same piece of it over and over again. He forced a calm self-assurance into his voice. "Here? In cold blood? In front of all these honest people? All these *armed* people? And me without a gun."

The expression on her face wasn't just a thunderhead look. It was a whole storm. He thought she must set a lot of store by that bay horse to feel so strongly about it. He could have been sorry it had been stolen. He might even have been willing to give it back to her—if only she'd yield a little. Not much. Just one damned decent word.

"I want Sundance," she said in a hard precise growl. *"Now!"*

He was thinking of her quick smile and the easy laugh. He thought of good food in a warm cheerful kitchen— and of men in the darkness driving long hard pain into his body.

She was a damn sight fancier liar than he'd ever be, he thought. Still grinning he said, "You promised me a horse, ma'am."

"Not Sundance! You got your horse."

"Yeah. That ain't all I got."

"I don't understand . . ." Shepherd began. But he realized no one was paying any attention to him. It was all between the woman and the stranger. It was something deeper than the loss of a horse. Something personal. Frowning, he watched them.

The girl said, "I should have killed you the first time I laid eyes on you."

"Maybe you'll get another chance," Loco answered. "But this ain't it. You go home. Go bake a cake or something. Only don't come back here with a bunch of men, thinking you're going to stomp on these people the way you done me."

"What?"

"You don't spring any more of your surprise bear traps, lady. Any tricks you try, we're gonna be ready for you. You come riding in here again, and you'll be riding into sight of a lot of loaded guns. *You're* the one who'll get bear-trapped next time."

"I don't know what you're talking about." She hesitated, waiting for some kind of explanation. But he didn't offer any. After a moment, she said, "I mean to have Sundance back. And I'll see you dead."

"Not today, lady." He drawled it with quiet certainty, even though it was all bluff. He had a notion she could have lifted that rifle to her shoulder, drawn a careful bead, and filled him full of lead, without a one of the settlers raising a hand to stop her. They stood gawking, holding their guns in their sweating fingers, looking as dumb as a bunch of sheep.

Ruth Caisson didn't seem to know that though. She wasn't seeing the blank faces that gazed at her. She glared intently at Loco.

The fire in her eyes smoldered down to embers of distrust. Wariness replaced her anger. And something besides wariness. Something searching. He wondered what it was she hunted in him with those sharp, gray eyes.

For a long, harsh, silent moment she stared at him in a way that was making him uncomfortable deep inside. Then, with a jerk of the reins, she wheeled the sorrel. Wordlessly she plunged it into a run. She didn't look back.

Loco watched her go, with a strange feeling of emptiness. Almost sorrow. He had wanted to fight *for* this woman, not *against* her. And he tried. Even now he knew he'd have given in to her, if she'd said one right word to him. But she'd made her choice.

"What's this all about?" Shepherd demanded.

Loco focused on the man facing him. The settler looked about as friendly as Ruth had. But there was no searching in his expression. His mind seemed made up as solid as rock.

Damn the man, Loco thought. He said gruffly, "I got a Caisson horse. And I got a bill of sale for a Caisson horse."

"She says different." Shepherd's scowl was all accusation. "I'd like to see the paper."

"Sure." Loco fingered into his pocket. He found nothing. With a frown of puzzlement, he grunted, "Your daughter washed these clothes. Maybe she seen it."

"I hope so," Shepherd grumbled as he turned. He called, "Essie!"

The girl must have been right inside the doorway. Rushing out, she gasped, "Yes, Pa!"

"You find a paper in my pocket?" Loco asked her.

The blush glowed in her face. Her eyes shone with excitement. If he could have taken hold of her and kissed her, he thought, she'd have come apart right in his arms. But he couldn't, here and now. And at the moment, he wasn't at all sure he wanted to.

She studied on it, then nodded. "It's inside. I forgot to give it back."

"Fetch it," her father snapped. He turned to Loco again. "You'd better be telling me the truth, boy."

Suddenly Loco felt a surge of anger, almost hatred for this little man with the soft, loose face and the damned determined tongue. What the hell business was it of Shepherd's whether or not he had a stolen horse? What right of any kind did the man have over him? Shepherd and his bunch were the ones who'd started all the trouble here in the first place.

The girl hurried back with the paper. She held it toward Loco, but her father snatched it out of her fingers. He unfolded it and squinted at it for what seemed to Loco like an uncommon long time. When he looked up, his face was still hard and suspicious. "That woman says a *bay* horse. This says a *dun*."

Loco shrugged.

"Which one you got? A bay or a dun?"

"What the hell difference does it make?"

One of the men bunched around spoke up. "I seen it. That other Mexican had it around here this morning. *Bay* horse with a Three-Slash-C on its side. Real handy-looking horse."

"That so?" Shepherd demanded of Loco. "You got the horse that woman says was stolen from her?"

"S'pose I have?" he snapped back. He didn't feel like palavering with this man. He didn't feel like doing anything much, except lying down. There was an unpleasantness in his gut, and his knees wanted to buckle on him. Leaning against the wall, he glanced across the faces peering at him. Why the devil should he care about these people, he asked himself. They sure didn't give a damn about him.

Shepherd pointed a stiff, blunt finger at him. "You answer me just one thing, seenyor. You answer me *yes* or *no*. You got a stolen horse?"

"Yes!"

There was a murmuring among the Sheep, like the crackling of a grass fire. And a stifling feeling in the air, like the fire smoke. Loco looked at the blurring images in front of him. He knew he wasn't going to be able to keep to his feet much longer. And he sure didn't want to fold up here.

Shepherd started to say something to him, but he wasn't listening. He *couldn't* listen. Shoving himself away from the wall, he balanced precariously on his feet and mumbled, "Go to hell."

It took all the determination he had to keep standing, keep walking back to the outbuilding. A heavy silence followed him. He'd shocked those Sheep. Upset them bad. He didn't care though.

At last he reached the shack and slumped down on his pallet. He lay on it, feeling it as if it were a hammock swaying under him. His heart was pounding hard. His lungs heaved for air. Still too weak to handle trouble, he allowed to himself. It wasn't a locked door or shackles that made a prisoner of him here. It was his own weakness.

Where was Ray now, he wondered. And the gun Ray had promised him? He might be needing that too damned soon. If Ray didn't get back in time . . .

Well, Ray wouldn't take kindly to it at all to get back and find these Sheep had lynched him, he thought. But it wasn't much consolation.

Dammit, they had no business getting riled about one stolen horse when they'd started it all with stealing other people's cattle. They'd done a murder, too, according to what he'd heard at the cow camp. Killed Ruth Caisson's father, the talk had it. What the hell business did they have condemning anyone else for anything?

But whether they had the right or not, he knew they did it. And it was going to mean trouble. He wasn't one of them. Shepherd had made that plenty clear. What was their punishment for an outsider who broke their laws?

Where the devil was Ray?

It seemed like there was always trouble of some kind lurking in the dark corners, waiting to jump a man when he wasn't looking, he thought wearily. He rubbed his fingertips at the scar over his eye, not aware that he was doing it. A smart man never hung around a place too long. Never got too set in one spot. Keep moving. There were plenty of other places in the world. Why care what happened in this one or what became of Ruth Caisson? Why give a damn?

He wondered if he should trust to fate and Ray deVaca or should try to get moving now, quick, on his own. He started to sit up, thinking if he could just hide out somewhere for a while, maybe it would be all right.

Footsteps sounded outside the shack.

Too late to hide, he thought, as he saw Shepherd framed

in the doorway. With a sigh, he leaned his head back against the wall.

Shepherd paused, seeming oddly uncertain. A judge about to hand down a sentence should be proud and confident, shouldn't he? Leastways, if he was right in his judgment.

But Shepherd didn't look very confident. Maybe he was scared, Loco thought. Only that didn't fit either. The man seemed more like he just plain didn't care for whatever decision he was going to pronounce. That didn't ease Loco's apprehension any at all.

With a defensive gruffness, Shepherd said sharply, "The council's met. We've augured it and voted. We've got to be bound by our own laws, else we'll fail in what we're trying to do here."

Loco didn't want speeches. He grunted, "Spit it out or swallow it."

Shepherd stiffened his spine. His jaw jutted from between his waddles. But his eyes stayed mild and there was a hint of request mixed with the demand in his voice. "You got to get out."

Was that *all?* No calling in the law? No surrender of the prisoner to Ruth Caisson? No back-yard lynching? Just leave? That couldn't be the whole of it, Loco thought.

He eyed Shepherd suspiciously, wondering what part of it was so distasteful to the man. What was the hidden hook? Tentatively he said, "Just get out? That's all?"

The soft sagging flesh of Shepherd's face creased in puzzlement. He seemed to have expected some kind of fight. It bothered him that he wasn't getting it. He nodded in answer, then he spoke. The words came out as if he were shy of admitting them. "I'm sorry for it, boy. If it was just up to me, I'd wait till you're better healed. But it's the council. We voted on it, and we *can't* abide having you among us. You got to go."

Loco was bewildered himself. He mumbled, "Right now?"

"No. You got till morning. By the time the sun clears the land, you've got to be gone."

"Else what?" he asked curiously.

"Else you'll be taken away."

"Dead?"

Shepherd sighed sadly. "If it comes to that."

"It won't."

Relief flooded the man's face. Sagging, he almost smiled. "We want to be fair with you. You've got to understand that. We'll . . ."

"Fair about what, my friend?" The voice was Ray de-Vaca's and it had an edge like a honed blade. He'd come up silently. Even Loco hadn't seen him there behind Shepherd in the doorway.

Shepherd flinched, but the fear only flashed in his eyes for an instant. The little man had strength of will. He stepped to the side, making room for Ray to enter. Half-turning, he drew himself up and faced them both. "Your friend is leaving in the morning. It's the decision of the council."

Ray rested the heel of his hand on his hip. The tips of his fingers touched his gun butt. He darted a quick glance to Loco as he asked, "Why?"

"He's a thief," Shepherd said.

"Huh?"

"I'll explain it," Loco offered.

Shepherd did smile with relief then. Gratefully, he nodded. But he remembered that he didn't trust this man. He asked, "There won't be any trouble?"

"Not of my making," Loco told him. "You go on, tend your chickens."

He hesitated. But it was easier to take Loco's word than to worry. He turned and hurried off.

Loco gestured for Ray to come sit down beside him.

"What's wrong?" Ray asked as he settled cross-legged on the floor beside the pallet. "I could feel it in the air like a hangfire when I rode in. Much trouble?"

"Nothing much. Just seems these Sheep can't 'bide a thief among them. So they want me to get out."

He shook his head, looking as if he weren't sure whether to laugh or explode.

Loco grinned at him, and set in to telling him what had happened. When he finished, Ray frowned warily and asked him, "You didn't let on *I* was the one who stole the horse?"

"No."

"Why not?"

"Hell, I'll be just as glad to be shed of these people and their fool war. Why should I get 'em mad at you, too? You got your job here. Do it and collect your pay."

"Ah, and share it with you, huh?"

Loco understood Ray's meaning well enough. He answered, "You do whatever you want. You don't owe me anything."

Ray laughed then. The wariness was gone. He said, "Dumb, stupid gringo. You're too damned clever. You know Ray deVaca don't *owe* nobody nothing, huh? Nobody corners him or pushes him. When he gives, it is with an open hand, huh?"

"I'm not asking you for anything."

"I know that. Maybe it's why I like you, crazy friend. But you're gonna need money, huh?" He fingered into a pocket. The coin he held up was a double eagle. "Here. Enough? Or you need more?"

Loco caught the flipped coin. "This is plenty."

"All right. Now you got money and you got a good horse. In my saddle pocket, I got a gun for you. You go somewhere and rest and wait for me, huh? When I'm done here, we'll ride together some more, huh?"

"Yeah." He turned the coin in his hand. Curious, he said, "Ray, how many of these would you want to kill me?"

For a moment, Ray studied on it. "Many. You are my very good friend. Like a brother. I wouldn't kill you cheap."

Loco grinned at him and pocketed the coin. It was

good to have a friend like Ray. One *honest* thieving killer was worth a settlement full of hymn-singing hypocrites who could rustle cattle themselves and yet damn a man for a stolen horse.

Leaning his head back against the wall, he asked himself why the devil he was even concerned over what these Sheep thought of him. There was no sense in it.

"You gonna be all right? Well enough to ride in the morning?" Ray said.

"Sure."

"What about the lady of the ranch? You want to get back at her? Maybe burn her house, huh?"

"No. Forget her," he answered. He smiled slightly, wishing he could take his own advice. But he knew it would be a long time before he got those gray eyes out of his dreams.

CHAPTER 10

It was still dark when Ray woke Loco. The lantern on the table burned low. Morning stillness surrounded them. Softly, Ray asked, "How you feel today, *amigo?*"

"Fine," Loco grunted as he sat up and stretched. There was some truth in it. A good supper and a night's sleep seemed to have helped a lot. The bruises were still plenty sore, but his head felt steady and his body strong enough.

"Will you fetch the horse, Ray?" he said. "I can take care of myself."

"Sure?"

"Yeah."

"All right." Ray grinned and headed out after Sundance.

Loco got the clothes on without any trouble. He slung the gun belt Ray had given him around his waist and buckled it. The gun was a Remington army model, forty-four caliber, with a ring on the butt. It set well in his hand. He had cleaned and loaded it the night before. And there were a dozen extra rounds in loops on the belt. Good enough, he thought, wondering where Ray had stolen it. Slipping it into the holster, he knelt and began to roll the quilt he'd slept under.

The sun was poking over the rim of the world when Ray brought the saddled horse to the door. Loco carried the quilt out with him. He was lashing it behind the cantle when he heard sounds inside Shepherd's cabin. He glanced toward it. Dammit, he didn't want to see the man again. He just wanted to get away from here without any more auguring or trouble.

But it wasn't Shepherd who came out of the cabin. It was Esther. She had a lumpy gunny sack in her hands. Pausing at the bottom of the steps, she held it out. Her smile was bashful, and she didn't meet Loco's questioning gaze. Almost stammering, she said, "I thought you might—could use this."

Ray asked, "What is it?"

She shot him a strange look, as if he were an intruder, and gave him no reply.

Loco ducked under the horse's neck and headed toward her. As he stepped up, she stared at the ground. Even in the thin morning light, he could see the blush spread across her face. Gently, he asked, "What is it, ma'am?"

His tone seemed to ease her shyness. She glanced at him. But she looked at the ground again as she answered, "Food. Some cheese and sausage and fresh bread and stuff. I thought—thought—"

"I'm obliged." He felt like he ought to say more than that, but he wasn't sure just what. The times and his feelings were all wrong for him to say what she wanted to hear.

As he took the sack from her, she brushed his hand lightly with her fingers. Her eyes met his. "Seenyor," she began. But she didn't go on.

Wordlessly, he turned away from her. As he walked back to the horse, she followed him. He pretended not to notice the way she hovered behind him as he started knotting the sack to his saddle.

Suddenly she spoke in surprise. "That's my ma's quilt!"

Maybe that was a way out, he thought. Keeping his back to her and his hands busy with the string, he grunted, "Yeah. I need one, so I'm taking it."

"But . . . !"

"I'm a thief. Remember?"

"No!" she protested, as if it were terribly important to her.

This was no good. This girl had no business building

herself calf-eyed dreams about him. He looked hopefully to Ray for help. But Ray only grinned, enjoying his discomfort. The girl was *his* problem.

He ducked under the horse's neck again and swung up to the saddle. As he found the off stirrup, the girl touched his knee. Her eyes were on him, imploring.

The horse was anxious to be moving, but he held a taut rein on it. Some other time and place, maybe, but not here —not now—only he couldn't just leave her standing there looking at him like that. He had to say something.

"I'm a thief," he repeated, wanting her to believe it. But she wasn't willing to. Not even with evidence of it in front of her. She kept gazing up into his face. Her fingers closed on his pants leg, clutching at it as if she could hold him there that way.

"No, please, seenyor, don't leave. . . ."

"I *got* to," he sighed. "Look, I'm being run off. I don't belong here. Don't you understand that?"

"No."

He realized that she really didn't. The only thing that made sense to her was the woman feeling she'd discovered inside herself. He had played a simple game with her. Nothing much. Just a grin, a touch, a few words. But they'd all been new to her. Now she wanted to learn the rest of the game. Only she didn't understand it was a game. She didn't understand at all. She thought the magic was his alone.

"Hell," he mumbled under his breath, thinking he damned well ought to stay away from preachers' daughters. Stick to women who already knew, who understood that it was only a game.

Her eyes pleaded with him. They hurt with the fear that he was the only one, and if he left, she'd never find him again.

The cabin door slammed open, its sound as sharp as a gunshot. Startled, he looked up. Relief mingled with the sense of danger as he saw Shepherd in the doorway. The man held a rifle. The muzzle jerked toward Loco.

The girl wheeled and gasped. Ray backstepped to cover at the corner of the outbuilding. And Loco's hand wrapped itself around the butt of the pistol on his thigh.

With his eyes on Shepherd, he opened the hand and spread it flat against his leg. He didn't think Shepherd would use that rifle, but he didn't trust little men with mild eyes who weren't accustomed to handling guns.

"Get away from him," the man snapped at his daughter.

She hesitated, looking desperately toward Loco. He knew she wanted the answer to come from him. He refused to give it. Reluctantly, she turned to her father then. And she obeyed, stepping away from Loco.

Shepherd came down out of the doorway. He paused, raising the rifle toward Loco's head. It was a fool thing to do. Even at such short range, the head was a small target. It could move more suddenly and further than the body. Add to that the trembling in Shepherd's hand and the wavering of the gun barrel. If he did pull the trigger, there was no telling what he'd hit. Most likely the roof of the outbuilding, Loco decided.

His first instinct of fear was overridden by anger. He was getting sick of this self-righteous little man. Holding the bay steady, he glared at Shepherd and said in accusation, "I'm not the only damned thief in this settlement."

The man didn't understand. He frowned uncertainly. "If you're missing something that belongs to you . . ."

"Not *me,* mister. The ranchers. They're missing a hell of a lot of cattle. And the Caisson woman's missing her father. You ever heard a word: *cojónes?* That's what you got. You and your hymn-singing Sheep."

Shepherd looked as if he'd been slapped in the face. His saggy cheeks quivered. They were turning a mottled red. His mouth moved, framing words, but he didn't speak them. Instead, he sucked a deep breath and sighed, steadying himself.

"Lies," he said very slowly and precisely, struggling to keep a lid on his anger. "All of it's lies. Damned ranchers' lies."

"Sure," Loco drawled. "That's why you want to hire a killer. To stop the ranchers from *lying* about you."

He'd slapped Shepherd again. Plenty hard. The little man was on the defensive now. Looking down at him from the height of the horse's back, Loco felt a vicious pleasure and a sense of power. He felt an urge to trample this smug hypocrite into the ground. They deserved it, all of these damned Sheep who would lie and steal and deny it, and then hire other men to do their fighting and dying for them.

"No!" Shepherd protested. He sounded pained. He seemed almost desperate to be understood—and believed. "No, not a *killer!* A *soldier!* A man to teach us how to defend ourselves. The ranchers want to destroy us."

"They got good reasons."

"It's all a lie. We've never stolen from them. We won't abide a thief among us. Not under any circumstances. We're people of the Lord."

Loco tugged the double eagle out of his pocket. He held it up. "I reckon these things just fall down on you from heaven, like rain?"

"What?"

"You're just a lot of simple, honest, poor Christian folk who take your living out of the land and never laid a hand to another man's beef, but you've got gold. Plenty enough of it to hire yourself a *soldier* like Ray deVaca, huh?"

"The money?" Shepherd muttered in puzzlement. Then slowly his eyes widened in understanding. "You think we got the money for stolen beef?"

Loco grinned at him in reply.

He shook his head. "No! We're—we—we came here to live a simple life. Some of us had lived in the sin of earthly possessions before, but we renounced such things. We sold all our sinful goods before we came here. The money went into a fund for community in case of emergencies. Blessed money to help us in time of sickness or want. Not stolen money. Not sin-stained! I swear it!"

Gazing into his face, Loco felt the anger fading. The man's eyes were sincere. They begged him to believe.

He glanced toward deVaca. Ray stood leaning a shoulder against the wall of the shed, watching with amused curiosity. As Loco looked toward him, he shrugged.

"I think he really means it," Loco said thinly. "It don't make sense, but it's true."

Grinning, Ray shrugged. He didn't much care where the settlers got their money, as long as they had enough of it.

"It *is* true!" Esther said, starting toward Loco's side again.

"Essie!" her father growled at her.

She paused, looking from him to Loco and back again, wanting the world to change somehow.

But the world hadn't changed. And Esther had reminded her father why he'd risen early this morning. He'd come out here to see that something necessary was done, that the will of the community was carried out. For a few moments, he'd been distracted, and the rifle had drooped in his hands. He lifted it and said firmly to Loco, "Sun's coming up."

The bright blaze on the eastern ridge was growing. Loco glanced at it. Whether or not the Sheep were thieves didn't matter. *He* was one. And he wanted to be clear of these people. Lifting rein, he nodded to Ray and said, *"Buena suerte."*

"Luego," Ray called after him.

The bay reacted eagerly, plunging into a gallop. Its hoofs clattered on hard-packed earth, sounding uncommon loud in the dawn stillness. As Loco turned it onto the wagon-rut road, he looked back.

Esther was standing with her hands out open in front of her. Empty hands.

He was sorry for that. She had been too simple, too vulnerable. He had never intended to hurt her. It had just happened. But pain came easy. Pleasure had to be hunted. Well, maybe she'd learn to defend herself against the pains and find the pleasures. He sure hoped so.

Dammit, it wasn't his problem, he told himself. But he hadn't meant to hurt her.

The bay covered ground with a bounding glide. Appreciating it, Loco thought as how there was magic in a horse. Somehow a man was taller, inside as well as out, when he was astride a good mount. The Mexicans understood that. Mexicans seemed to understand a lot of things that gringos generally didn't. Ray had understood his need of a good horse as more than just a way to cover ground.

This was one helluva fine horse. It was easy-gaited enough not to strain the sore muscles over his gut, and quick enough on the bit not to pull at his bruise-circled wrists. He could sympathize with Ruth Caisson's concern over losing it. Served her right though. She was responsible for the bruises.

It occurred to him that it might not be exactly safe to get himself spotted riding Sundance. Likely as not, she would have ordered her men to shoot him on sight if they saw him on this horse. Or if they saw him any whichways. A woman who'd have a man buffaloed and beaten like that probably wouldn't hold off any on having him killed, either.

It might be a good idea to stay to cover until he was well away from this part of the country, he decided. Do his riding up in the rough high places where there was plenty of brush and woods. Lots of gullies and outcrops where a man could hide himself and his mount quick if he had to.

The land on three sides of the settlement lay open. He swung the bay off the wheel ruts, heading toward the wooded slopes of the western ridge. As he reached them, he slowed to an amble and opened the gunny sack. He broke off a piece of the fresh bread. Chawing on it, he looked out at the rolling land.

The breeze brought him scents of the rising mists, of spring grass and sun warmth and a bright new day. A good day, he told himself. If a man had a good horse, plenty of food, and some coin in his pocket, what else did he need?

But still something dark lurked at the edge of his mind. It nibbled at his enjoyment of the morning like a rat. For a while he fought it. But then he allowed to himself that he wasn't really done with this basin and its troubles. He didn't know just how or what would keep him involved here, but he could feel it as sure as he could feel the tender soreness still in his belly muscles. There was more trouble yet to come.

Trouble behind and trouble ahead. Well, let it come when it pleased. He'd worry about it when he could see what shape it meant to take.

The strange thing was that he didn't feel inclined to try to outrun it. There sure wasn't any sensible reason to want to hang around this neck of the woods, especially not after the way Ruth'd had him beaten. But—dammit—he wanted to see her again. He wanted to try once more. . . .

It'd never work, he told himself. Stay away from her. But still . . .

He mulled over his thoughts, auguring himself as he rode higher into the rough country. He was heading for the safety of quick cover. But he was heading back in the general direction of the ranches and the cow hunt as well.

Despite the easiness of the bay's gait, he was beginning to ache. And he was getting tired. Too tired too quick. The sun hadn't yet reached the top of the sky when he decided he wanted to rest awhile.

He could hear water rushing somewhere nearby, and Sundance scented at it with interest. He headed in search of it. How long would it take to get over that beating, he wondered as he rode. The bruises felt like they went clear through to his backbone. How much good would he be to himself when trouble did arrive?

He found a deep gully cut by the runoff of spring thaws.

Its sides were steep, about man-high. Fresh water gushed in a fast stream at the bottom. The bay sniffed eagerly and tugged at the bit. But Loco didn't feel like jolting down the steep bank. He turned to follow the stream and hunt an easier way down.

He found what he wanted. Upslope a ways the water had undercut the bluff, toppling a mass of earth down into itself. The fallen land was mushy, but the slant of it was gentle. He headed Sundance onto it.

The horse took high, cautious steps, its hoofs sinking into the mud and making small sucking sounds as they were lifted out again. They left impressions that filled quickly with water and would soon disappear.

Drawing rein at the water's edge, Loco stepped down. He hunkered to catch his hands full of water and drank deep. Then he rubbed his cold, wet hands across his face. As he blinked his eyes open, he looked at small water-filled pocks along the edge of the stream. Another horse had been here not long before. A ridden horse, he thought. This might not be a very good place to stop for a rest. He glanced back the way he had come. That was when he saw the boot.

It lay at the base of the bluff, and it was the color of the clayish mud, but its shape was plain enough. Stepping over, he squatted to look closer at it. The color was soaked in as if it had been buried in the earth a long time.

But the mud had been scraped off. A high-heeled rider's boot for a foot bigger than his own. A fairly fancy one, with a pattern stitched into the side in the shape of a brand.

Three-Slash-C.

Touching it lightly with one fingertip, he remembered the talk he'd heard. Ruth Caisson's father had ridden out one day last fall and had never been seen again. Had he been wearing this boot?

He looked up at the face of the bluff and the slough of earth that had been broken from it. Small lumps like clay-clovered bits of rock lay in the mud near him. He reached for one and thumbed at its coating of mud. It wasn't rock.

He rinsed it in the stream and studied the small, gnarly bone. Letting it slide out of his fingers, he got to his feet. He wiped his hand down his pants leg, then rubbed at the scar over his eye.

This might answer one question. It might tell him where Caisson had disappeared to. But not *how* or *why* or whether it had been an accident or murder.

Gathering the bay's reins, he stepped to the saddle. This was definitely *not* the place he wanted to rest awhile. In fact, he wasn't feeling nearly as tired now as he had been. Excitement was stirring in his blood.

He wondered what would happen if he rode to the Three-Slash-C with this news. And who was it who'd been here just before him? Who had wiped the mud off that boot, then left it lie?

Turning the bay upstream, he scanned the ground for sign of the other horse.

CHAPTER 11

Loco winced, startled by the shot. He knew it hadn't been meant for him. It hadn't sounded very far away though. Rising in the stirrups, he peered ahead. There was nothing to see but woods.

The horse under him tensed and tossed its head. To it, a shot meant a hunt. Sundance was eager to run. But Loco held a taut rein as he listened.

The gun snapped again. It sounded like a rifle. Another rifle answered it.

Warily, Loco eased rein. He moved Sundance slowly into the woods. It was only a thin strip of forest. It stopped abruptly. The land fell in a sharp slope down a ragged wall scattered with brush and outcorps of rock to a wet-bottomed canyon.

Halting the horse within cover of the woods, he scanned the canyon. A man knelt in the brush at the base of the far wall, holding a rifle to his shoulder. Beyond the man, half-hidden around a bend of the wall, Loco could see horses. Two of them, under saddle, dragging their reins. As he watched, the man's rifle sputtered smoke. The crack of the gunshot echoed thinly.

The gun that answered was on this side of the canyon, upslope, hidden among the scrub and rock. Nudging Sundance forward slightly, Loco caught sight of the smoke. A pale puff of it had risen on the roar of the shot. The wind was already whipping it away. As he hunted its source, he saw a brownish mound in the brush. A downed horse.

The rifleman on the floor of the canyon fired again. And the one hidden upslope answered again. This time Loco spotted the source of the powder smoke. He saw the patch of velvet green that blended with the brush but wasn't quite the same. He had seen that shade of green before. It was the color of Ruth Caisson's riding suit.

The range was no good for a pistol, but that was what he had. It was already in his hand as he considered the possibilities. He scanned the canyon, hunting a man who might belong with that second horse down there.

Movement caught his eye. Then a glimpse of color. Something was slithering through the brush toward the girl's perch. A man in a dark shirt, bellied down and crawling like a snake. From where she was, the girl wouldn't see him. He was closing in, moving upward to get above her. He meant to fire down on her.

The dead horse lay on a faint trace that Loco figured was a game trail working its way to the canyon bottom. He took a moment to judge the ground between it and himself. Not good footing, but enough for a really nimble horse. He hoped.

All right, you damn-fool horse, show me you're as good as you think you are!

Leaning low over the pommel, he slammed his heels into the buffalo pony's sides. He didn't need spurs. Sundance was eager to run. Stretching out its neck, the horse sucked at the scent of burnt powder and plunged at an angle down the slope of the canyon wall. It ran like the devil's son. It scrambled over rough earth and slid rump down as it hit a sharp drop. Catching balance, it ran again without a break of stride.

With a touch of the rein, Loco swerved it onto the game trail. The footing was better here. The bay's stride stretched out even further. It flew. Straight toward the man bellied down in the brush.

Loco gave a scream, with a sound like a panther.

The man rose up, startled fear in his face. On his knees, he stared at the rider bearing down on him.

Loco felt the buck of the Remington in his hand. Lead lost itself somewhere in the bushes. He fired again, this time knowing the shot was closer.

He saw the kneeling man lifting a pistol, steadying it in both hands. He felt his own gun jump a third time.

The pistol pointing toward him spat smoke.

Above the pounding of his blood and the hammering of the bay's hoofs, he heard both shots blend into a single roar.

The man on the ground frowned as if he'd just discovered something he couldn't quite understand. His head tilted forward.

Loco fired again. Almost on top of him now.

He jerked as if he'd been kicked. Half-rising, he stumbled, then toppled backward into the brush. The rush of the horse carried Loco on past him.

There was no more threat from that one. Loco swung the horse downslope. His eyes hunted the rifleman who had been on the canyon floor.

A fool-crazy headlong attack could be effective in more ways than one. He'd seen it work before. It could rattle hell out of whoever was being attacked.

He glimpsed a leg swinging across a saddle on one of the horses upcanyon. Both animals disappeared at a hard run.

Grinning to himself, he eased back and hauled rein. The bay was lunging forward fast. It took several strides to slow and finally to stop itself.

He grabbed for the saddle horn. The horse stopped all right, but his head didn't. It spun wildly. Mumbling a soft curse, he closed his eyes and caught a deep breath. When he looked up again, the world was steadying. But his head still felt wobbly. With a gentle flick of the rein, he turned the bay to head back up the slope. Slowly.

Lead spanged past him.

"Hey!" he hollered. "Stop that! Hold off, bosslady!" He scowled at the patch of brush where he knew Ruth Caisson was hidden. Dammit, he'd just hauled her bacon out the ashes. The least she could do was leave off trying to kill him.

She fired again.

He whipped Sundance around, ducking low over the pommel and cursing. Ought to leave her walk home. Serve her right. But she was a long way from the Three-Slash-C up here. As far as he knew, she was a long way from anywhere. And—dammit—he *wanted* to see her. He'd never have a better excuse. . . .

He rammed his heels at the bay's flanks. At a gallop, he zagged it upslope toward her.

She threw another shot. But it went far wide.

"Hold off, bosslady," he shouted. "Don't shoot!"

She fired again.

Again it was a far miss. He wondered if maybe she didn't mean to hit, but just to scare him off. It was a reassuring thought. He wished he believed it.

He was closing in. Close enough now, he decided. Leaning back, he eased the pace. As he pulled rein, he swung himself out of the saddle. The horse was still moving as he jumped. He hit ground running.

A couple of long strides took him over the low ridge of rock in front of her position. He swerved to one side of the gun barrel that pointed toward him. With a lunging jump, he went through the brush. He jerked himself to a halt at her side. And his knees folded up under him. He fell flat on his face.

Digging his fingers into stone and gravel, he hung on. The earth pitched, pumping and yawing under him. It tilted sharply, as if it meant to go down and roll on him. For a terrible moment, he thought it had him beat. But then it slowly settled back until at last it lay motionless under him.

His gut ached as he sucked air into his lungs. Groggily, he raised his head. The girl was a blur in front of him. At least she seemed to be sitting still, not leveling her gun at him. He dragged himself up onto one arm and caught a deep breath.

His voice came hoarse and shaky. "Bosslady, I ain't in no shape for this kind of games."

"Loco?" she said thinly. She sounded as if she didn't believe it. And she sounded scared.

"Yes'm." He tried squinching his eyes shut, then opening them slowly. This time they almost focused. He saw her face, as pale as moonlight, with the eyes deep-set shadows in it. He saw the rich velvety green of her jacket dunned with dust. And smeared with a dark ugly stain.

She'd been hit! The realization jolted him into sharp awareness again. He scrambled to his knees.

She was sitting up, leaning her back against an upthrust of rock. The rifle lay with its action open and empty beside her. Her hands were limp in her lap. She gazed uncertainly at him.

Not hit bad, he thought hopefully. The stain was high on her left shoulder. He reached toward her.

"Keep away from me!" she screeched, throwing up her right hand. She clamped it around his wrist, wrenching hard. Her fingers bit into the tender bruised flesh on his wrist.

Yelping, he winced. She'd startled him. And she'd hurt. With a twist, he pulled free of her grip. He sat back on his heels, frowning at her as he rubbed the sore wrist.

She held her hand up in front of her face like a claw to defend herself.

"Bosslady, I'm sick of getting hurt trying to help you!" He felt a temptation to mount up and leave her here. But he knew he wouldn't.

She looked over the defensive hand at him. Vague and puzzled, she said, "Hurt?"

"Yes'm!" he snapped, shoving the sleeve up his arm. The flesh around his wrist was still a dark mottled purple, spreading to a sickly yellow. He held it up toward her. "You think that *don't* hurt?"

"I don't understand," she mumbled. Her hand still hovered in front of her face.

"You people around here don't understand nothing! You have a man beat all to hell and you get set on kill-

ing each other off and maybe you think you know why,
but you don't. You don't understand one damned thing.
Bosslady, I don't know how bad you're shot, but I got a
notion it'd be a good idea to try and stop that bleeding.
You want help or don't you?"

She shook her head slowly. Her eyes were glassy. They
seemed to be staring straight through him.

He realized that she was dazed. She might not even
be aware that she'd been shot. He knew that could happen at times, in high excitement. Sometimes the hurting
didn't begin until a while afterward.

"Ma'am, I don't want to hurt you." He spoke gently
this time. "I mean to help you, if you'll let me."

She shook her head again.

Cautiously he held a hand out toward her, coaxing as
if she were some timid animal he wanted to lure. He repeated it softly. "I don't want to hurt you."

"You're one of them," she said.

"No, ma'am."

"The Sheep hired you to fight us." She paused, hunting
some thought. "I saw you there. You work for them."

"No, ma'am. They ran me off. They think I stole your
horse. They won't 'bide a thief among them." He searched
her face, wondering if she understood what he was saying.
"They're not the cattle rustlers you're looking for, either."

The fear in her was easing some. Her hand lowered
itself. But it hung over her lap, still ready to fend him
off if need be.

"You've got to stop the bleeding," he said.

It took her a moment to understand what he was talking about. She raised the hand toward her shoulder.
Lightly she touched the stain. Then she looked at her
fingertips. Very softly she said, "I think I need help."

"Yes'm." He moved closer to her. She was watching
him with wary uncertainty. As he reached to unbutton her
jacket she grabbed his wrist again.

He winced at the sudden pressure on sore flesh, but

this time he stopped himself from jerking away. She was scared enough now. Quick moves would just spook her worse.

Quietly he said, "Don't do that, ma'am. I only mean to help you."

Her fingers opened themselves slowly. She whispered, "Promise?"

"Yes'm. I swear it."

Resting her head against the rock behind her, she dropped her hand into her lap. Her eyes closed. And the tips of her teeth dug into her lower lip.

She flinched as he touch the top button, but she didn't fight him. She sat there as rigid as the rock she leaned against.

Carefully he opened the jacket and turned it back from her shoulder. Under it she was wearing a plain white cotton blouse. More blood smeared it, sticking the cloth to her skin. The wound looked to be high, close to the collarbone. She didn't hunch as if the bone were broken, though.

"It don't look bad," he muttered as he reached for the blouse buttons.

She shuddered, suddenly flinging up her hand. She didn't grab at his arm, but she shoved it away.

"No!" she moaned, sounding pained. Her eyes were clenched tight. He could see tears beading at the corners of them. Her chin was quivering.

It wasn't the pain of the wound, he thought as he sat back on his heels. It was just plain fear. She was the proper-raised kind. She would almost sooner die than have him see her and touch her under that blouse.

"Hell," he grunted. He wiped at his face with the back of his hand. This wasn't so easy for him either. Not when he intended to keep the promise he'd made to her. He damned well didn't want to hurt her in any way that she might never forgive. But how did you do anything for a wound you couldn't touch or even look at close?

"Can you use your left hand any?" he asked her.

She opened her eyes enough to squint at him under the lashes. Slowly she lifted her left hand. This time it wasn't fear that knotted her face. Moving that hand hurt her.

"Easy. That's enough," he said.

She let the hand rest in her lap again, but pain still drew her face taut. And a fresh reddening showed on the blouse. Stirring had wakened the wound.

"Bosslady, you can't help yourself," he told her. "And I can't help you without I touch you."

She eyed him through her lashes. Faintly she said, "My blouse—off?"

He considered. It looked like the wound might not be bad. He suggested, "Maybe I can just tear out a piece over the bullet hole. That do?"

She pressed her good hand to her breast under the wound. Reluctantly she said, "I think so."

"All right." He glanced at the skirt crumpled around her. "Only first I'm gonna have to have one of your petticoats for bandaging."

"No!" she sounded as if he'd proposed something downright indecent.

"Well, it's either that or my shirt. And I figure you got more'n one petticoat, but this is my only shirt."

Studying him narrowly she said, "Would you?"

Her voice was husky and soft. It asked a lot more of him than the words did. He sighed, not sure whether he was proving something to her or just plain giving in to her. With a shrug, he started to untie the leather lace that held his chaparral jacket closed.

"Turn around," she said. "I'll get a petticoat off."

He turned his back to her, listening to the rustly sounds of cloth and thinking thoughts that didn't help any at all.

"All right," she said at last.

When he turned toward her again, she was sitting the same as she had been. But she held a wad of white cloth out in her right hand. Her eyes were open. Not vague and glazed now, but bright with pain.

"Hurts bad?" he asked as he took the petticoat.

"It feels like there's a hot poker stuck through my shoulder."

"Yeah." He knew the feeling.

"I understand now why the calves bawl so at branding time." She gave him a strained smile.

"They got worse than that to cry over," he muttered as he ripped at the petticoat. "Leastways, the he calves do."

When he looked up at her, the smile was gone. Her face was set hard, the eyes closed tight, and the mouth a thin line. She had leaned her head against the rock again. Her hand was pressed protectively to her breast.

"If it ain't bad, I'll see can't I bandage it without I tear up your jacket," he told her. "I'll do this the best I can. I promise."

She nodded slightly. Then her lips moved in an almost inaudible, "Thank you, Loco."

He pinched together a fold of the cotton above her hand and started the rip. Carefully, he opened it toward the bloodstain. Dried blood pasted the cloth to her skin. His fingers trembled as he peeled it away.

She shuddered, choking a groan in her throat. He wasn't sure whether it was from pain or that deep-bred fear.

"What you doing up here?" he asked, hoping talk would distract her thoughts.

She licked at her lips, then said hoarsely, "Was on my way up to Bremen's."

"Who were you shooting at?" With a piece of the torn petticoat, he dabbed at the moist blood. The hole was under the arch of the collarbone.

"Rustlers. Moving a gather," she answered. "I saw them."

"Good enough to recognize any of them?" He touched the bone gently. It felt solid enough. That was a piece of luck. Collarbones usually broke easy.

"No. I don't—don't know all those Sheep by sight."

"I told you it ain't the Sheep," he said, swabbing at the wound again. The hole seemed clean. The blood didn't flow or spurt. It just oozed, and that was a real good sign.

Meant she wasn't losing too much of it too fast.

"What?" she muttered.

"The Sheep ain't stealing your beef."

She winced and gasped as he prodded lightly around the wound. Taut, she bore the touch and the hurting. His fingers found a lump. It wasn't deep. Too far to get at without a probe of some kind though. Dammit, if he'd had a knife, he could have taken it out here and now.

He told her, "You must have been near out of range when you were hit. You're hardly hurt at all."

"I *feel* hurt."

"Sure. I guess you never been shot before. Take my word for it, bosslady, you got started real easy." He pressed a pad of cloth against the hole. "Can you hold this here?"

She inched up her hand, trying to put her fingers over the pad and hold up the torn blouse at the same time. Swallowing hard, she said, "You *know* it's not the Sheep?"

"Yes'm," he grunted as he stretched out a strip of cloth.

Carefully, he threaded it up under her jacket. "You got to lean forward some."

She did. He slid his hand up, carrying the cloth between the jacket and her back. His arm was around her, his face very close to hers. He could feel her breath against his cheek. Dammit!

He caught the end of the bandage over her shoulder in his other hand. Jerking his arm away from her, he sat back on his heels. He was going to have to take another wrap of the bandage around her. But first he had to catch his breath. We wiped at his face with the back of his hand.

He'd been talking to distract her. He hoped he could do as much for himself. "Bosslady, if you ranchers go attacking them Sheep, there's gonna be a lot of people getting hurt and maybe killed, and it's all one hell of a mistake."

She eyed him narrowly. "Loco, are you talking around corners again?"

"No, ma'am, I'm telling you the straight of it. The Sheep ain't the ones you want."

"Then who?"

"I don't know. But I know the Sheep ain't thieves. They don't 'bide thieves among them."

She didn't know whether to believe him or not. That showed in her face. Hesitantly she said, "You stole my horse."

He sighed, wondering if there was any chance at all that she'd believe him if he explained that. Afraid it would just complicate things worse, he decided not to try right now. He told her, "That's got nothing to do with them. Excepting that they ran me out of the settlement on account of it. That's how they feel about thieving."

She frowned, troubled at her own thoughts. After a moment, she said slowly, "We are planning to attack them. We're gathering in the morning. That's what I was riding up to see Mister Bremen about. To ask him and his men to join us."

"Hell," he muttered. "You *got* to call it off, ma'am. It ain't no good. It's all wrong."

Her voice was thin, still uncertain. "Loco—please— the truth?"

"Yes'm. I swear it." He wished he could find a way to convince her. From the way she gazed at him through her lashes, he knew she wasn't ready to accept his word for very much. But his word was all he had to offer.

CHAPTER 12

When he'd finished wrapping the bandages, Loco made a sling for the girl's arm. He tied the knot with trembling fingers. It wasn't easy being so close to her without doing anything about it.

Her gray eyes were on him, still questioning him. There was trust in them, but not much of it. One wrong move, maybe even a wrong word, and it'd be gone. It'd never come back again. And that wasn't the way he wanted things.

Sitting back on his heels, he rubbed his sweating palms down his thighs. He drew a deep breath, feeling the tenderness in his belly muscle, and told himself he was in no fit shape for more than thinking anyway.

"How you feel now?" he asked her.

"It hurts."

"Just ignore it. It'll stop after a while.

"Is that what you do?"

"Sure," he grinned. "Bosslady, we'd better get you somewhere you can be doctored proper. You think you can stand up?"

She nodded.

"I'll fetch the horse over here." He started to his feet. And suddenly there was no strength in him at all. His head reeled. The world spun around him. His knees began to buckle. With a thin whistle between his teeth, he eased himself down again—before he fell. Sitting, he sunk his wobbly head into his hands.

"Loco? Are you all right?"

"Yes'm," he mumbled, his voice muffled by his hands.

"You're hurt?" She sounded concerned. But he supposed that was only natural. She was depending on him to get her home from here.

"No, ma'am. I'm just tired. Wore out. Got to rest a minute more."

She was watching him in thoughtful silence. He could almost feel her gaze. After a long moment she said, "What happened to your wrist?"

The question surprised him. She should know well enough what had happened. But he answered her. "When your hired men beat me up they tied my hands. Kinda tight."

"When *what?* I don't understand."

Was it possible that she really didn't? He wondered if there could be any other explanation for that beating. Lifting his head slightly, he looked through his spread fingers at her. His eyes didn't want to focus. Trying to make them do it only got his head to feeling worse.

Concentrating, he said, "That night I ate at your house, you set that bear trap for me, didn't you?"

"I don't know what you're talking about." She sounded honestly puzzled. And that puzzled him.

"After I'd ate and I went outside, what do you think happened?"

"I don't know. You left and went to the Sheep settlement, didn't you?"

"Bosslady, somebody jumped me in your bunkhouse and hauled me off into the woods and beat hell out of me. Then they dumped me at the settlement. If it wasn't at your orders, whose idea was it?"

Indignant, she started. "You think *I* would—I—Loco, I didn't know anything about it!"

His head was settling down. His eyes sharpened her image. The look on her face was sincere. Believing her, he grinned behind his hands. He made his voice mockingly solemn. "You swear that to me, bosslady?"

"Yes!"

"Then who you reckon done it? Who else had reason?"

She lifted an eyebrow at him. "Everybody! Mister, you cut a swath coming in here. Within twenty-four hours you ruined Coosie's pies, shamed Deck in front of his own men, made a fool of me, and stole Ronny's saddle. And heaven knows what else. What do you expect?"

He rubbed at his face with his hands, then looked at her. "You figure I earned it?"

She didn't answer that.

"Well, maybe I did," he owned, grinning. "But they didn't have to damn near kill me."

Darkly serious, she said, "They think you're the hired killer that the Sheep sent for."

"You still think so, too?"

She gave it some thought before she admitted, "I don't know."

"Well, I ain't," he said, starting to rise. But the giddiness surged up fresh. Settling to the ground again, he muttered, "No good."

"They did beat you! You're still sick from it, aren't you?"

"I'm tired," he insisted. The feeling was a lot like just plain exhaustion. He knew the beating was the reason for it, but he didn't want to own that to her. He hurried on to say, "Look, this Bremen, he's the one who didn't want to make trouble for the Sheep, ain't he?"

"Yes. Loco, you . . ."

"Is his place far?"

"We're on his land right now. I . . ."

"And you figure he's at home?"

"He rode up from the cow camp yesterday. He should still be there," she answered. Before he could interrupt her again, she rushed to say, "Loco, I'm sorry for what happened. If I'd had any way of knowing . . ."

"Forget it. Look ma'am, maybe I could take you on to Bremen's place. Get you patched up. And he could do the running around. Would the rest of the ranchers listen to him and hold off their attack?"

"Yes. We don't *want* a war. If there's anything—any kind of proof at all—everybody will be glad to hold off fighting."

"Proof," he mumbled, afraid there wasn't anything better to offer than his own word. He pressed his face down into his hands, trying to concentrate. There was a thought hovering at the edge of his mind. But he couldn't catch it. He was tired as hell. His eyes didn't want to stay open. Couldn't let himself fall asleep though. Too much to get done. He had to get Ruth Caisson to someone who could help her. Had to get the bullet out of her shoulder. Had to stop a war . . .

Jerking open his eyes, he lifted his head. He squinted at the girl, seeing that she was asleep. Then he realized he'd been asleep himself. For a couple of hours, to judge by the sun.

Cautiously, he tried standing up. This time he made it. His head didn't feel so much like it was going to fall off, and his eyes stayed open. Maybe the siesta had been worth the time it used up. And Ruth probably needed rest just as much as he did. He wondered how far it was to Bremen's place and how hard the ride would be on her.

Sundance hadn't drifted far. Loco spotted the horse upslope a ways nibbling at green shoots. He approached warily, not wanting to spook it.

It eyed him suspiciously, but it obeyed the dragging reins. He caught them and grinned. "Maybe you wanted some rest too, huh, fella?"

The horse nudged him in the arm as he led it back toward Ruth. He halted it, then knelt and gently woke her. "We got to get moving, bosslady."

She frowned groggily at him. Her face was very pale. Lifting her good hand, she clutched at his sleeve. "Loco?"

"Yes'm. Come on, you *got* to wake up."

She tried, and she made it most of the way. But she was vague again, the way she'd been when he had first reached her. He had to get her standing up on a rock, work the horse over to her side, and then pretty much lift her into the saddle.

Once she was on board, he swung up behind her. As he reached around her to pick up the reins, his arm brushed her side. She flinched, going tense.

"You're not still afraid of me?" he asked.

She shook her head.

"Then what's wrong?"

She was silent for so long that he decided she wasn't going to answer. Gigging the horse, he headed it up-slope. She sat rigid in the saddle in front of him. As they reached the top of the bluff, he halted and asked again, "What's wrong?"

She glanced over her shoulder at him. There was a tinge of color on her pale cheek. In a small, almost-shy voice, she admitted, "I've never ridden astride before."

"Is it that bad?"

"It—it's not *ladylike*."

He didn't mean to laugh at her, but he couldn't help it. "Bosslady, you're wonderful. You think nothing of running a ranch and bossing a crew same as a man. You ride all over the countryside by your lonesome like one. You even take to shooting at people and getting shot back at, like a man. But then you get all upset and blushy about setting a horse like one."

"I—I guess it is kind of silly of me."

"Yes, ma'am."

"But—it's—I—" Her voice trailed off. He realized then that it wasn't just straddling the horse that bothered her. *His* presence had a lot to do with it. Fear wasn't the only feeling his touch stirred in her.

Grinning, he bit his tongue, then said, "You just take it easy, bosslady. You relax, or you'll be all wore out before we ever get to this Bremen place."

"I don't feel very good now," she answered. "I don't know if I can ride far. I'm awfully tired."

"Lean back and rest against me. I'll keep you on the horse all right."

"No!"

He sighed, telling himself it was better not to augur her. "How do we get to Bremen's place?"

"Road over there." She gave a nod. "Then that way, right to the door."

"I'll find it." He lifted rein again. "If you get tired, just lean back."

She mumbled something under her breath. It wasn't long before her head slumped forward and she swayed in the saddle. He closed his arms around her, drawing her back against his chest. The weight of her leaned on bruised flesh, but it was hardly painful. Not at all.

Her head nestled against his shoulder and neck, her brow pressing warmly on his cheek. She slept softly in his arms. He thought dreamily as how it would be damned pleasant to sleep like that, with her snuggled up against him. Right now his eyes wanted to close. His head leaned lightly against hers. So easy to drowse. So pleasant . . .

Yeah, and then we'd both fall off the horse, he told himself.

The bay was plodding. He picked it up into an amble, wondering how much farther to Bremen's. Where was that wagon road anyway? He sure hoped he wasn't lost. But he didn't want to waken Ruth to find out.

Before long she woke of herself. He felt her start. Her body stiffened and her head lifted from his shoulder.

"It's all right, bosslady," he said softly, wanting her to stay relaxed in his arms.

She pulled away though. Leaning forward, she wrapped her good hand around the saddle horn and shook her head against the dregs of sleep. Hazily, she mumbled, "Loco?"

"Yes'm?"

"Am I still dreaming?"

"No."

"I was, though."

"What about?" he asked.

She didn't answer him. Instead, she said, "Who are you, Loco?"

"Just me."

"*Loco* isn't a name."

"No, ma'am. I told you before, I ain't got a name."

She considered that in silence. She seemed to still be groggy from the wound. He figured that was natural enough. He still felt the effects of that beating himself. Right now, he was a mite lightheaded and plenty tired.

Curious, Ruth tried asking, "Where do you come from?"

"I don't know."

"You have to come from somewhere."

"Bosslady, I don't *have* to do much of anything, except what I take a mind to."

She laughed very softly. "Have you taken a mind not to come from anywhere?"

"I figure that don't matter much. It's more important where I'm going." He could see the trees thinning out ahead. The wagon road at last, he thought.

"Where *are* you going?"

"Bremen's."

"You know what I mean," she insisted. "Where are you going?"

"Hell, I don't know. I'll find out when I get there."

She tilted her head forward. He wasn't sure whether she was thinking or going to sleep again. But as they reached the wheel ruts, she stirred and said, "That way."

He turned the bay uproad, in the direction she pointed. He wished she would lean back and fall asleep again, the way she'd been before, but she seemed to have wakened more instead of drifting off. After a moment, she said, "I've been trying to place you by the way you talk. I can't, though. It's sort of mixed up."

Grinning to himself, he thought as how it wasn't just his way of talking that was mixed up. Why were people always so eager to put labels on each other, he wondered. He asked her, "What does it matter where I come from?"

"I'm just curious," she said as if it didn't matter at all. But then she added, "You're hard to make sense of. And the way you talk all around the barn doesn't help. I guess I—I'd like to understand you better."

She sounded sincere. It made him feel almost obligated to give her some kind of straight answer. Reluctant, and a little embarrassed, he said, "I don't know. A city somewhere, I think. Maybe St. Louis or Memphis or Cairo or some one of them."

"How can you not know where you come from?" She didn't say it like she was doubting him. She just didn't understand.

"I remember cities and I remember stowing on boats to get out of one and on to another. That's all. The small towns weren't no good. They'd catch you too easy in 'em."

"Who'd catch you?"

"I don't know," he said again. He felt like a damned fool. But it was the truth. The memories from that far back came to him in vague, broken pieces. They were more just *feelings* than anything else. Mostly he recollected being scared or hungry or cold, or all of them at once. And he remembered rats. Rubbing his fingertips at the scar over his eye, he concentrated. He wanted to call up some kind of answers for her. But the memories were only dark icy shards that didn't make much sense.

Suddenly there was a word in his mind. Funny sort of word. Thinking it gave him a shuddery feeling. He said it aloud, *"Asylum."*

"What?"

"Asylum. What's it mean? You know?"

"A sanctuary," she said blankly. That was no help. But then she suggested, "A refuge. A place of safety."

"Like hell," he grunted. "They lock you up and try to beat the devilment out of you."

Suddenly she was tense again. Even worse than before. She glanced over her shoulder at him, and there was something like terror in her eyes.

"What's the matter?"

"Loco . . ." She said it as if all of a sudden it had a

lot of new meanings for her. And none of them good.

He couldn't understand why, but he knew that it was *him* she'd got so bad scared of. Back off and let her calm again, same as a spooky horse, he told himself.

Drawing rein, he slid from the bay's rump. He stepped up to its head and looked at Ruth. She stared at him as if he were a rattler in the road, coiled to strike.

"I don't know what I done wrong," he said.

She didn't answer.

"If you think you can get on to Bremen's alone, maybe you'd better." He offered the reins up to her, though he didn't want her to take them.

She looked from his face to his outheld hand, then back again. And she took the reins.

Sighing, he stepped out of her way, meaning to show her that he wouldn't stop her. And hoping she wouldn't go.

Again, he said quietly, "I don't know what's wrong."

She almost started the horse. But even as she lifted the reins, she tugged them. The animal danced uncertainly and tossed its head. It was ready enough to move on. But Ruth hesitated.

Loco could see that she was drawing a tight rein on herself, struggling with her sudden fear. Her eyes searched his. She swallowed hard. Her voice came ragged and thin. "*Asylum*—a place where they locked you up—but you ran away?"

He nodded. "Yes, ma'am. Do you know what I'm talking about?"

"Don't you?"

"No. It was a hell of a long time ago. I wasn't but a little kid then. That's all I remember about it."

"A k-kid?" she stammered. Suddenly she was crying. She clutched the saddle horn, leaning forward and sobbing. And laughing at the same time.

He couldn't make sense of her at all. Feverish from the bullet wound, maybe. She'd dropped the reins. He caught them close to the bit, steadying the horse. Laying his other

hand against its withers, he looked up in question at Ruth.
He sure as hell couldn't leave her like this. He didn't know
what to do.

She lifted her head and met his eyes. Tears streaked
her face. She brushed at them with her knuckles, then
smiled at him. The fear was gone.

Snuffling, she said, "I'm sorry. I thought—thought—
Loco, would you take me on to Bremen's—please?"

Whatever had been wrong, it was past now. Bewildered,
but glad, he swung up behind her and put the horse into an
amble.

"Are you sure you're all right?" he asked the girl.

"I'm fine," she said faintly, glancing back at him. He
saw the color in her face. It seemed more like a blush
than fever. Her small smile looked embarrassed. "I—I'm
sorry for what I was thinking. I misunderstood."

"I got no idea what you were thinking," he told her.
"I got no idea what I was talking about. Just a piece of
a memory."

"An *orphan* asylum. It *must* have been."

"I guess so." At least he knew what an orphan was and
that fit. He sure wondered what she'd had in mind. Not anything good, he judged. He didn't want to chance upsetting
her by asking about it though. The important thing was that
she thought different now. And she did that all right. It
was in more than just her words. He could sense that somehow things between them had changed a lot.

"I'm sorry," she repeated.

"Forget it. You just take it easy. We'll be to Bremen's
pretty soon."

"Um hum," she murmured, nodding. And then she was
leaning back against his chest. Not asleep this time, and
not at ease. But doing it of her own will. She nestled
against him, her head on his shoulder.

With a strange certainty, he knew this was the first
time she'd ever rested in a man's arms this way. Before,
she had always been the one who dominated, who con-
trolled any situation. She had never yielded, never trusted

in this way. She had never before given herself over to a man's protection.

Grinning to himself, he held off the temptation to snug his arms around her waist. Take it slow. Don't spook her. This was enough for now—this warm softness of her and the knowledge that she had come to trust him this far.

There was something here *he* had never known before, too.

CHAPTER 13

Through the thinning trees, Loco spotted a small log house. It sat in the middle of a broad field. The wheel-rut road led from the woods across the slope and up to the door. From there it wound on to a cluster of outbuildings and corrals. The buildings had that same deserted look as the Three-Slash-C. Bremen's crew was out on the cow hunt. Loco hoped Ruth wasn't wrong about someone being at the ranch.

Nudging the bay's flanks, he hurried it toward the house. As he approached, he glimpsed a figure in the shadowed doorway. It hesitated, then disappeared back inside.

Loco shouted a hallo.

In a moment a man came out of the cabin. It was the wiry, sharp-eyed old hawk he remembered from the cow camp. There was a rifle in Bremen's hands. His boot-leather face wrinkled into a scowl behind the lush, gray mustache. He called, "What the devil's this?"

"She's hurt," Loco answered as he halted the horse. He didn't wait to be asked down. Sliding from its rump, he offered his hands to Ruth.

He had to help her from the off side. Wrapping her good arm around his neck, she half-climbed, half-fell from the saddle. He caught her and put his arm around her waist, holding her against him.

"What's this?" Bremen asked again. He eyed Loco with suspicion and added, "What have you done to her?"

"She's been shot. By rustlers."

"What?"

Loco didn't feel like wasting time in talk. Ignoring the man, he started toward the cabin. He would have carried the girl—would have liked to—but he didn't have the strength for it. With his arm around her, supporting her, he walked her to the door.

For a moment Bremen just stood frowning at them and running a hand over the action of the rifle. Then he ducked ahead of them on into the cabin. As Loco brought Ruth through the door, he was lighting a lamp.

The front room was a rough-hewn parlor with Indian blankets flung over home-built furniture and sets of antlers racked over a big empty stone fireplace. Loco helped the girl to the sofa facing it.

"Shot by rustlers?" Bremen said, holding the lamp up in his hand. He peered at Ruth's face. "Did you see them? Could you identify them?"

She shook her head.

"This is bad. This changes the whole situation," he muttered thoughtfully. Then he shot a sharp look toward Loco. "What about him?"

"He's my friend," she answered.

It was taking Loco some effort to stay on his feet. He felt washed out, bone-weary, ready to fold up where he stood. He asked, "You got any drinking likker around here?"

The question seemed to startle Bremen out of some deep thought. The rancher squinted at him for an instant, then put down the lamp and hurried off. He came back with a bottle and a couple of glasses.

Loco took the bottle. Uncorking it, he drank deep from it. The whiskey was good stuff. It went down with a smooth warmth and began to spread pleasantly into his body. He took one more swallow, warning himself that too much would do him more harm than good. Dammit, he wished he could lie down right now. Rest now and worry later. But there were too many things to be tended first.

Dropping to one knee at her side, he offered Ruth the bottle. She shook her head.

Bremen grumbled something in his throat and thrust out a glass. Annoyed, Loco tilted the bottle over it. But

Bremen didn't drink it himself. He held the glass toward Ruth.

Suddenly Loco felt wrong and out of place. He looked at the girl questioningly.

"You drink this, Missy," Bremen was saying. He put the glass into her good hand. She closed her fingers around it, but didn't lift it.

"It'll help," Loco suggested.

She gazed into the glass, then slowly raised it and sipped. Suddenly she was coughing. It racked her, bringing tears to her eyes.

"Whoa, there," Bremen said soothingly. He reached for the glass. As he took it, she pressed her hand to her throat. She gasped as if she were choking. At last, she got her breath. Thinly, she said, "That's worse than getting shot."

"Sorry," Loco mumbled. He sure hadn't expected it to hit her like that.

When she moved the hand away from her neck, Bremen reached out. He caught her slender fingers in his gnarled crusty ones and stroked them gently. She looked into his face and smiled.

The burning in Loco's gullet wasn't from the whiskey. He swallowed at the surge of anger, not sure whether it was this damned old silvertip he hated or himself. He knew that the mistakes, the wrongness, were his. But Bremen was sure no better, he thought. The damned old coot was fondling her hand when he should be worrying about her wound.

"You got somebody around here as can take the bullet out of her shoulder?" he growled.

"I can," the rancher answered.

The hell with that. Anger overrode the weariness. Loco swung to his feet. He was taller than Bremen. That helped. Looking down scornfully into the rancher's face, he said, "If you ain't got a *woman* on the place to do it, I'll do it myself."

Bremen's eyes were flint and steel. They snapped back

sparks of distrust and dislike. He slid a hand into a pocket. Bringing it out, he held up a silver dollar. "Here. For your trouble. I'll take care of her now."

"Loco!"

Ruth's voice was startled—and scared. For an instant, Loco didn't understand at all. Then he realized his hand had wrapped itself around the butt of his pistol. It was halfway clear of leather.

Letting the gun slip back down into the holster, he unpeeled his fingers. He wiped the empty hand self-consciously across his face. This was no good. Acting this way would just make the wrongness worse.

Bremen glowered at him. The threatening move didn't seem to have bothered the little man at all.

"Loco." Ruth spoke softly this time. Her eyes were on him, a little frightened, a little pleading. "Would you tend to Sundance?"

So he was dismissed—like that—*hey, boy, take care of the horses*—likely she'd be offering him money in payment next. Wheeling, he strode out of the cabin.

He picked up the reins and led the bay around back. Jerking off the saddle, he turned the animal into a small corral. It rolled a couple of times, rubbing its sweaty back into the dust.

Loco crossed his arms on a fence rail and leaned his head against them. He closed his eyes, letting the weariness that was in him wash at the anger. They mingled into a sense of discouragement. He became aware again of the sore aching in his bruised belly muscle. And he thought of Ruth's gray eyes, serious and sincere, as she claimed she hadn't known anything about that beating. He thought of the feel of her in his arms, and his own certainty then. What was the lie and what was the truth?

Something tickled at his ear. Jerking his head up, he saw Sundance shy back from the sudden move. The horse had been nuzzling him. It studied him through sorrowful horse eyes. Tentatively, it stretched its neck toward him.

"All right, old horse," he muttered, reaching to scratch

at the sweat marks the bridle straps had left on its cheek.
"You and me, huh? We get ourselves some rest and then
we light out together. Get the hell away from here, huh,
amigo?"

But that was no good either. If something wasn't done
to stop it, a war would bust loose in this basin tomorrow.
A bunch of self-damned fools would be killing each other
off for a lot of wrong reasons.

He tried telling himself it was none of his business, but
it felt like a lie. He had made it his business by knowing
it was wrong. He was the one who could do something
about it—maybe. At least, he could try.

The horse lipped at his hand, wanting more scratching.
He gave it an affectionate shove and turned to stalk back
to the cabin. *Hey, hombre, the next time they offer you
money, take it. It's damned well all you'll get. Yeah.* There
was strength in anger. He nursed it. With his fists clenched
at his sides, he strode into the front room.

Ruth was sitting on the sofa with a blanket over her
knees. She had the jacket off now. Blood stained the crude
bandages he'd wrapped around her shoulder. Bremen
had put a basin of water on the floor, near her feet. He
was pulling a straight chair over toward her. As Loco came
in, he dropped it.

No one spoke. Loco reached for the whiskey bottle.
He uncorked it and took a long swallow. With taut de-
liberation, he stoppered it, then set it down again. He
turned slowly to face the two of them. They were staring
at him.

"Somebody ought to bury that poor bastard I killed for
you," he said to Ruth.

She looked at him as if he'd hit her.

"And somebody ought to do something about all the
rest of the people who are gonna be getting killed around
here," he went on. "Only the ranchers ain't gonna listen
to *me. You're* the only one as can stop it now."

"What the devil are you talking about?" Bremen
snapped, glaring at him.

Ruth clutched at the arm of the sofa. Her fingers dug hard at it, the knuckles drawn pale. She turned toward the rancher. "Mister Bremen, you've got to stop them!"

He grunted, not understanding.

"The ranchers," she said. "Everybody's meeting in the morning. They're going to attack the settlement. They've got to be stopped. They're all wrong. The Sheep aren't the rustlers, the way we thought."

The boot-leather face twisted into a wary scowl. "If they ain't, who is?"

"I don't know," she admitted.

"Then what makes you so sure it ain't them?"

"I just *know* it," she answered with a quick glance toward Loco.

He nodded agreement, wishing he had proof of some kind to offer. There was an idea shaping itself in his mind.

"On *his* word?" Breman said as if he couldn't believe it.

"I know it's true," Ruth insisted. "I found where—where my father was buried. Up near your boundary. I wasn't far from there when I glimpsed a rider. I started after him and I saw them. They were moving a gather in that wet canyon. . . ."

"Yeah," Loco interrupted. "They got a gather. And if they got good sense they'll break it up and scatter now. But maybe they ain't got good sense. Maybe they'll try to hold it. If they do, all you've got to do is get everybody on this range up there hunting them and their sign. You'll catch 'em all right. Leastways, there's a good chance of it. Catching them will do you a damn sight more good than a shooting war with a bunch of fool hymn singers who never done you harm."

Bremen's eyes narrowed to thoughtful slits. He stood motionless, studying on it. Then he nodded. "All right, Ruth. On your say-so. I'll take care of everything. I'll send Harry up to the cow camp right now."

"Mister Bremen, I wish you'd go yourself," she said. "I know they'll listen to you."

"Missy, I got to get that slug out of your shoulder before it sets to fester."

"Loco can do that. Please, Mister Bremen, go to the cow camp."

He considered for a moment more. Then he nodded again. Stepping to the inside door, he hollered, "Harry!"

A voice answered gruffly from inside the cabin somewhere. "Be there in a minute, boss."

"No, just go out and saddle me a good horse," Bremen called back. "I've got a hard ride tonight."

"There should be a full moon," Ruth offered apologetically.

"Don't you worry about it, Missy." Breman gave her a stiff smile. It looked like a poor fit on his rocky face. He turned to Loco. "You take care of her."

"I'm gonna need some stuff. A knife and clean cloth and some carbolic acid, if you got it. If you ain't, I'll make do with the whiskey."

"I'll get 'em." He scurried off, suddenly friendly and helpful.

Relieved, Loco faced the girl. She gazed at him with uncertainty. He hung onto the anger that was strength. Harshly, he asked, "It all right with you?"

She nodded. Her face was very solemn.

Bremen brought in the stuff Loco had asked for and set it all out on the straight chair. With a gruffness that tried hard to be gentle, he said, "Missy, soon as he's done, you better get some sleep. I'm leaving Harry here. He'll look out for everything while I'm gone."

He turned to Loco then and added, "You can bed in the bunkhouse. Harry'll show you where."

The voice of the hired hand rattled through the cabin. "Got your horse ready, boss."

"Don't you worry none, Missy," Bremen said as he started off. Loco heard him telling the hand, "I got some things for you to tend to while I'm gone. . . ." Then a door slammed. After a few moments, he could hear a horse start off at a gallop. Maybe everything would be all right, he thought. Leastways, for the Sheep. He turned to Ruth again.

As he started to peel away the bandages from her shoulder, she asked him, "Will it hurt?"

"Yeah. I can't help it. I'll do it as easy as I can." He spoke with a terse sharpness.

"What's the matter?"

"I wish I knew."

"Loco . . . are you mad at me?"

"No."

"But you are angry?"

He looked into her face, and suddenly he was grinning. "Hell, bosslady, if I don't stay mad, I'll fall asleep."

She smiled at him. Reaching out, she wrapped her hand around his. She clung as if she had to hang on. Her eyes closed. Softly and intensely, she said, "Thank you, Loco."

The temptation to kiss her was almost overwhelming. He might have given in and done it. But she opened her eyes again. With determination, he set himself to the task at hand.

The bullet must have been nearly spent when it struck. It hadn't broken bone, but had gone straight into muscle and buried itself there. Probing gently with the knife, he brought it out whole. Hardly flattened at all. No shattered pieces of lead or bone splinters to worry about. And Ruth hadn't even hollered as he got it out, either. He felt an admiration for that.

He swabbed the wound thoroughly with watered carbolic acid, washing away the bits of cloth and dirt the slug had carried with it. There wasn't much bleeding. All in all, it was as clean and simple a bullet wound as he'd ever seen. As he bound fresh bandaging over it, he told her, "That shouldn't give you no trouble."

Her face had been clenched into a tight knot. She opened it slowly. Tentatively she asked, "Is it over?"

"Yes'm."

"It wasn't so bad." She sounded surprised.

"No, ma'am. It wasn't in deep. Good clean hole. Shouldn't hardly leave a scar." He tied the final knot, then rubbed at his face.

Relaxing, she looked at him with drowsy curiosity. "You've got a scar over your eye."

"Huh?"

She reached out her good hand and touched a fingertip to his brow. "There."

"Yes'm," he mumbled. He never gave it any particular thought. When he did, the memories that roused up were dark and damned unpleasant. Better forgotten.

"Is it a bullet scar?" she asked. Her voice was soft and deep in her throat. He could see the drooping heaviness of her eyelids. And he could feel his own trying to close.

"No, ma'am," he said. "I think you better get comfortable and get some sleep now."

"All right," she murmured.

He helped her to stretch out on the sofa. Taking a blanket from a big chair, he spread it over her. Her eyes were already closed and her mouth relaxed into a gentle hint of a smile.

Cautious of anything that might disturb her sleep, he turned the lamp low. Then he reached for the whiskey bottle. It became a dim blur in front of his eyes. As his fingers touched it, he felt them shaking. His strength had run out. His knees felt about to fold up on him again. Getting a grip on the bottle, he settled to the floor.

He sat there, fighting to stay awake long enough to get himself a drink. The cork felt like it was glued in. Holding the bottle with both trembling hands, he pulled it with his teeth, then spat it away and tried for the whiskey.

Some of it went down his chin. But enough went down his throat. He felt the mellow warmth of it spreading in his gut. Setting down the bottle, he rested his head on the edge of the sofa. His eyes were closed, and he knew he couldn't open them if he tried. He was vaguely aware of

something touching his head. Without awareness, he
sensed the girl's fingers twining in his hair. They rested
there, as if reassuring her that he was still beside her. He
slept in deep, warm contentment.

CHAPTER 14

It was a warmth, a gentle darkness, a dreamless rest. But then the sound crept in and it became icy night. The sound of four small feet and a bare hard tail tap-tapping on the wharf. The boy who huddled behind a windbreak of cotton bales woke suddenly and afraid.

He jerked back his head at the instant that the unseen rat lunged. With the numbness of shock, he only vaguely felt the sharp chisel teeth sink into the ridge of his brow. He knew nothing but the angry fear that filled him. The squirming thing hung in front of his face. His hands closed over it, jerking. He didn't feel the teeth as he tore it away, or the struggling claws scraping at his hands. There was a stinging in his eye, but he wasn't aware of the blood.

He held the thing clenched in his hands, squeezing until it wasn't struggling any more. It became a limp skin-bag of mush under his fingers.

Rising, he flung it as far and hard as he could. He heard it splash somewhere out there in the frosty night-dark that lay over the river.

For a time he just stood, thinking that there were more of them somewhere in the darkness. Lurking, waiting, ready to attack. It was only slowly that he became aware of the pain and of the blood that streamed down his face.

In the dim grayness that came before dawn, he set out to find a horse trough full of fresh water so he could wash the blood away. But a brass-buttoned billy loafing under a street lamp spotted him and started after him. The nabber chased him all to hell and gone before he finally found a hole where he could go to ground.

He had huddled there in the new darkness, listening, knowing that there would be more rats. More dark things in dark places, ready to attack.

He heard the small tap-tapping of four clawed feet and a bare hard tail. . . .

Jerking awake, Loco was suddenly alert. He made no move, but listened tensely. Most of it had been a dream. The sound was there though. Not a padding rat. Footfalls. Someone coming into the cabin from the back. Someone trying hard to move noiselessly.

He told himself that it was probably either the hired hand or Bremen back again. Whoever it was simply didn't want to disturb the girl sleeping on the sofa. All right— but it was such a furtive sound—and the feeling of the dream was still cold in his veins. He wasn't thinking of the gun on his thigh, but his hand wrapped itself onto the butt. It drew the gun gently from the holster and let it rest hidden at his side.

Hinges spoke softly as a door was edged open. The careful footsteps were coming into this room. Holding motionless, Loco looked toward the door through slitted eyes.

The lamplight was too low. He couldn't make out anything about the dark figure that paused in the doorway. But he could hear the shallow, nervous breathing. And he didn't like it at all. He didn't like the way the man came slowly into the room. *Sneaked in,* he thought. Too damned much like a rat in the dark. What business did he have in here?

He came toward the sofa.

Loco's thumb rubbed gently at the cocked hammer of the Remington. Through his lashes, he watched the man come toward him, then halt and look down thoughtfully. The lamplight gave shape to one side of his face. Not Bremen. Not anyone Loco remembered ever seeing before.

A thick-set man with light shaggy hair and a stubble of pale whiskers on his jaw. His forehead furrowed in a

deep frown and his mouth was hard-set. His right hand
hung shadowed at his side. As he moved it, his shoulder
twitched.

Loco glimpsed the gun in his hand.

His own hand jerked up, snug on the Remington. There
was no hesitation—no thought—only the instant. As the
barrel leveled toward the man's chest, the hammer fell.

The flare of the gunshot in the dimness filled Loco's
eyes. Its roar slammed into his head, echoing inside it,
overwhelming every other sound. He didn't hear the man's
startled grunt. Or Ruth's small sharp gasp. Only the roar
and the dull pounding of his own heart.

The powder smoke stung in his nose. The glare left a
green gray haze in his eyes. Through it he saw the gun
that had risen toward his face waver wildly. The hand
that held it shook, then opened, as the man was flung
back by the impact of lead. The gun fell skidding across
the floor. The man staggered, his empty hands groping. He
bent forward, then fell, tumbling into a limp heap. Still
and silent.

Dead, Loco thought.

Something clutched his shoulder. Wincing, he flicked
up the muzzle of the Remington. The hammer was at full
cock under his thumb.

But it was Ruth's hand that had clamped onto his
shoulder. He jerked down the pistol, hoping he hadn't
frightened her with it.

She was sitting up, holding onto him with her right hand.
The lamp cast long deep shadows across her face, but
they didn't hide the fear that was in it. Or in her voice.

"Loco! What's happening?"

"It's all right," he said, not sure how else he could answer her. He wasn't certain what had happened himself.

Her fingers had dug deep into his flesh. Slowly they
eased their grip. He could sense that she was drawing up
strength from somewhere within, steadying herself. The
hand relaxed, then pulled away from him.

He rose to his knees and reached out to prod at the

body heaped in front of him. He'd been right. The man was dead. Sighing wearily, he lowered the hammer and put down the revolver, then rubbed his hand across his face. The dampness was only sweat but it seemed sticky, like blood. He felt a dim urge to find water and scrub the stickiness away.

"What happened?" Ruth asked again. This time there was a calm acceptance in her voice. At the sound of it, Loco felt a moment of almost amused astonishment. Shooting and death didn't frighten her nearly as much as her own feelings did.

"I'm not sure," he told her.

"Is he dead?"

"Yeah."

"Who is he?

"I don't know." He raised the flame, then picked up the lamp. Reaching out, he turned the body face up and held the lamp close over it. "You know him?"

"No," she whispered thoughtfully. Then, with a gasp, "Loco, I *think* he's the other man who was shooting at me out there!"

"The hell!" he grunted. That might make sense. The rustler could have spotted them coming to the ranch and followed them. He might have been lying in wait outside, looking for a chance to get rid of them. But would he have let Bremen ride off that way?

And where the devil was Bremen's hired hand, Harry?

He was supposed to be around, looking out for things. He'd sure have heard that shot, wouldn't he? He should be hurrying to see what was wrong, shouldn't he?

Unless the dead man was Harry . . .

"You sure you don't know him from anywhere else?" he asked the girl. "Not from around the range or the cow hunts or anything?"

"I'm sure."

"You know all of Bremen's hired men?"

"No, not all. Hired men come and go."

"Yeah." He set down the lamp and took a swallow from

the whiskey bottle. "What about this man, Harry? You
know him?"

"No," she muttered, watching him punch empty car-
tridges out of the Remington. As he started to reload, she
asked apprehensively, "Loco, what are you thinking?"

"I think *this* is Harry." He gestured toward the body.
"And I'm wondering whether Bremen went to the cow
camp, or maybe he took my advice and went to make
sure the rustlers break up that gather and scatter."

"Mister Bremen?"

He nodded. "Every other rancher I heard talking
down to your camp wanted to fight or something. Put an
end to the rustling somehow. Bremen wanted to keep
things going along just like they have been. And he talked
about lending money. You owe him money, bosslady?"

"Some. I don't understand."

"If he's taking your beef and turning a profit on it, he'd
want to keep on that way as long as he could, wouldn't
he? Then when you go bust, and he can't steal off you any
more, he could start claiming your land against the money
you owe, couldn't he? 'Sides, if he was getting robbed, the
same as you, where would he be getting all that money to
lend to you anyway?"

"Yes," she said slowly and uncertainly. "But . . ."

He stuffed the loaded gun back into his holster as he
got to his feet. Offering her his hand, he told her, "Bosslady, I don't think we ought to hang around here waiting
to find out. I hope you feel up to riding a ways."

She accepted his help. He could sense that the weakness
of shock from the gunshot had passed. She might still be
a little wobbly from the loss of blood, but she should be
able to get along.

"I'm fine," she said, meaning it.

He grinned at her, glad that she had sense enough to
know her own strength. "Come on."

He led her through the cabin to the back yard. The
moon was full and high, washing the land with its stark
white glow. Shadows black as pitch wavered in a thin

breeze. The horses in the corrals stood sleeping. Leaving
Ruth leaning against the rails, he went to catch Sundance.

Once the bay was saddled, he got a rope on a dark trim-
legged geld and threw a saddle from Bremen's barn across
its back. He tied it by the reins and went to help Ruth
mount up.

She settled into the saddle. As he held the reins up to
her, he caught a sound. Poised, he listened.

Growing, the noise became the clatter of hoofs on hard-
packed earth. Horses, several of them, coming closer at an
easy lope.

"Is there time enough for Bremen to have got to the
cow camp and back?" he asked in a hurried whisper.

"I—I don't think so."

"All right, bosslady," he muttered, grabbing the bay's
reins up close to the bit. Turning its head, he led it into
the blackness beside the barn.

"What's the matter?" Ruth said.

"Maybe nothing. I don't know. You may have to do
your riding alone. You wait here. *Don't move.*"

"But what . . . ?"

"I'm going out and meet our company. If it's friends,
I'll be right back. If it ain't, you just wait here until you
can't hear hoofs no more. Keep waiting awhile after that.
Then you light out for the cow camp, fast as you can
ride. You hear?"

"But Loco . . ."

"You understand me, bosslady?" he demanded. The
riders were getting closer. They would be clear of the
woods soon. He had to hurry. But he had to be sure she'd
obey him.

She started, "But *you* . . ."

"I'm good at running and hard to catch. I'll lead them
for a hell of a ride," he answered, pulling loose the geld's
reins. As he stepped up to the saddle, he added intensely,
"You got a war to stop. Don't mess around. You hear?"

"Yes."

The geld wanted to shake out a few kinks. Keeping its

head high, he rammed his heels into its sides. It lunged
into a run. He glanced back, but he could see nothing in
the shadows where Ruth was hidden.

The riders appeared on the road where it came out of
the dark forest. Five of them. Vivid figures in the moonlight, grabbing rein on their mounts as they saw a man
galloping toward them. For a moment, none of them understood. They hesitated.

Friends or enemies—Loco couldn't be certain. But he
didn't mean to take any chances. They were too much like
rats poised on the edge of the darkness, ready to attack.
He kept low over the pommel, holding the Remington in
his hand.

"Bremen!" he hollered.

The voice that responded wasn't speaking to him. It
called to the horsemen. "Get him!"

So that answered that. Bremen wasn't taking any chances
either.

Swaying, with a jerk of the reins, Loco swung the geld
sharply. He zagged, swinging back again, as lead sang
past him. A helluva target, moving erratically through
the moonlight, but even so he wanted the protection of
the forest. And he wanted to lead those riders after him.

They were all startled, all excited. He hoped none of
them would pause to think and stay behind. To add to
their confusion, he snapped a shot toward them.

They realized they were bunched too close. Spreading,
they raced after him. Another fast-thrown slug slammed
past him as he reached the edge of the woods. He plunged
the geld into the shadows.

He had to slow as he wove through trees he could
barely see. Too damned dark to make any time in here.
He headed the horse toward the twisting wagon road.

On it, he hit into a run again. The sound of the geld's
hoofs would tell the riders behind him that he was on the
road. They would know where to chase after him. But they
might also know how to cut him off. He hung to the
road a short ways, then wheeled into the woods and halted.

Hoofbeats told him that at least some of the pursuit
had taken the road after him.

He wished he could remember the ride up here better.
Usually he had a good eye for such things. But on the way
to Bremen's, his attention had been on the girl. And he'd
been so damned tired then. Still tired. And not sure about
the turns of the road. At a walk he worked through the
forest, hoping he'd short-cut a bend and come onto the
wheel ruts again.

Behind him, he heard a holler. Someone had realized
he was back in the woods.

The moonlight was bright enough to hunt a man by,
but not to hunt his sign. He wondered what Bremen's
crew would do if they lost him. He didn't intend to find
out though. He had to make sure they stayed on *his* trail
while Ruth Caisson rode to the cow camp.

When he found the wagon road again, he broke the
geld into a run, calling them with its pounding hoofs.
Iron shoes clattered on packed earth somewhere behind
him in reply.

He played the same game over. But the next time that
he made it onto the road a rifle spanged lead at him.
Somebody had thought to try heading him off.

The geld stumbled as he wheeled it toward the shadows. With a jerk, it caught itself. In the same instant, he
heard the rifle snap again. Lead whined close past his
cheek.

Snorting, the geld lunged into the woods. It slammed
into a thicket. As it hesitated, he lashed its rump with the
rein ends. Dammit, now he *needed* spurs. But the horse
answered the sting of leather, crashing into the brush.

He was aware of the riders behind him. He could hear
them moving through the woods. They were spread out
now, working among the trees like Texans in the brasada.
He realized that they were herding him. Herding him as
if he were a *ladino*.

Those men knew the countryside. Enough moonlight
trickled through the trees to give them some vision. And

they knew where the lay of the land would force him to change direction. They knew the cuts and gullies and bluffs. They'd head him out of the forest onto the moon-swept open.

He was aware that the forest was thinning around him. Not much farther to open country, he thought. And not a lot longer until the beginning of dawn. He'd make a real fine target out on the rolling plain with the sun brightening the sky behind him, huh? He shivered at the notion.

It seemed like everything was running out on him. He could feel the horse wearying. He paused to let it blow, knowing from the sounds in the woods that they were catching up with him. And so was that beating he'd taken. He could feel the ache in his belly muscle again. His wrists were sore from playing the geld's reins. And his head felt too light again. A little drunk. Not so pleasant as drunk though. Now what do you do, you damned fool, he asked himself. Somewhere behind him a branch cracked.

He felt an urge to drop off the horse and send it packing. They'd chase it. He could lie still in the brush as they went by. Yeah. Then he'd be afoot, a long way from anywhere. And they'd catch up with the riderless horse quick enough. They'd be back here hunting him again.

There were too many ways of knowing where a man was. If you couldn't see him, you might still hear him. Or scent him. Or even stumble over him by accident.

He had five shots left in the revolver. Six, if he took the time now to reload that empty chamber. But there were five men after him. Even fully loaded, the gun would only allow him one wasted shot. So unless luck were riding his shoulder, he'd be stuck trying to reload an empty gun while someone crept up on him. And right now, he had a feeling he'd left his luck a long way behind somewhere. It'd be no use holing up and hoping to hold them off.

The sounds were closing in. *All right, hombre, you think you're so damned clever—do something!*

He jabbed his heels at the geld's sides, urging it on.

Nowhere to go but straight ahead, into the open.

The Sheep settlement was out there somewhere, across a long, long stretch of open land. He didn't think he could make it. But he couldn't think of any alternative.

Just run like hell and hope a lot.

Through the trees, into the grassland. Running hard now. There were dips and gullies. Stay to the low places. Don't get skylit if you can help it. Don't wear out the horse either. It's a long way yet.

A rifle screamed at him.

Hooking a leg, he lay himself against the geld's side, away from the woods. The horse was a big-enough target. He didn't want to add himself to it any more than he had to.

The rifle called to him again. Close. Whoever fired it wasn't on the rocking back of a horse now. He thought they had stopped up there somewhere near the edge of the woods. Letting their mounts blow. Trying for a good clean shot. Stay alive, *hombre*, you're gaining ground now.

But he could feel the horse flagging under him. Not a lot of run left in it. He'd covered a fair piece of ground this night. He was back where he'd been this morning. He'd been riding easy then, favoring sore muscles and taking pleasure in the bright promise of the day. Now he was riding like hell and wishing day would never come. Dammit, the horse didn't have much left. Not enough to get it to the settlement. He felt sure of that.

He wasn't sure about the sky. It seemed to be turning a little pale. The smell of the rising dawn was plenty clear though. He could catch scents of the freshness that came before the first touch of the sun. A new day on the way. Bright and shiny, scented with green grass and warm sunlight. Yeah. And pretty soon the smell of earth turned for a new grave?

Against the skyglow, he glimpsed the faint forms of buildings on a rise far ahead. Small dark blocks clustered together. Sheep huddling for protection. Where was their sheep dog this morning? On the alert for wolves? Damn you, deVaca, if you're comfortable asleep. . . .

The geld faltered. Behind him, Loco could hear pounding hoofs. He felt the twitching of his mount's weary muscles. He had started with the fresher horse, but they'd worked him like a beef, herding him, taking turns breathing their mounts while he'd had to keep his moving. Now it was the geld that weakened.

He figured they knew this would be happening. They'd be expecting him to go down. Then they'd unlimber their guns again.

Not much more, horse. Just enough. Please.

But hoping wasn't enough. He felt a swaying, not sure whether it was the exhausted animal beginning to weave, or his own head reeling. Whatever it was, it was costing him ground. He could tell that from the sounds of the hoofbeats behind him. *Por favor, amigo . . .*

Somebody tried a rifle again. Hell trying to hit a moving target from a running horse. A man had to be damned lucky, or it was a waste of lead to try.

This one was damned lucky.

As he heard the third shot, Loco felt the geld lurch. It stumbled and he knew it was going down. Too soon, he thought with despair as he flung away his stirrups.

He threw himself from the saddle. His shoulder hit ground first. Clutching the revolver, he rolled.

The horse made a couple of strides before it spilled. It collapsed into a heap.

Loco lay bellied down in soft dirt and grassy stubble. He could hear the harsh rattle as the horse tried to gasp breath. It had been headed upslope when it fell. Lifting his head, he could see it in the dawn glow. It bent its forelegs, trying to raise itself. But it pitched forward, sprawling again. Its breathing was pained and ragged, gurgling from lungs that were filling with blood.

Flattened in the grass, he squirmed toward it. He could hear the hoofs of pursuit, and feel their hammering in the ground under him. They were slowing down. Spreading out, too, he thought. They knew they had him. They'd be closing in now like the jaws of a bear trap.

The sounds of galloping stopped. They knew he was armed. He supposed they'd move in slowly, not taking any chances. He didn't bother to look.

The struggling horse was aware of him. Tossing its head, it snapped long teeth at him. There was light enough now for him to see its mournful eyes filled with pain. Why did horses look so sorrowful? What did they know about life that a man didn't? He grabbed its forelock and pressed the muzzle of the Remington to its face.

The shot snapped sharp and thin in the softness of the rising morning.

That leaves you four rounds in the gun now, *hombre chiflado*. And there are *five* men out there, ready to take your hide. Well, you've got more loads in the belt loops for what good it'll do you.

Lying pressed against the body of the dead horse, he lifted his head. He found that he was in a hollow. Grassy hummocks rose around him. He couldn't see far in any direction. He couldn't see anything of the men who had chased him here. Couldn't hear them either. What the devil were they up to, he wondered. They sure knew they had him pinned in this hole. And they wouldn't leave without making certain that he was dead, would they?

They were just taking it easy, he decided. Likely waiting now, breathing their horses and letting him wonder what was going on. If he showed his head to find out, he'd be game in a turkey shoot.

He lay still, catching his own breath. Let *them* wonder what *he* was up to.

Damn you, deVaca, what kind of general are you anyway? Within sight of your damned settlement—why don't you have guards out here keeping watch—why the hell aren't you here to haul me out of this hole?

No good, he owned to himself. He'd tried to get close enough to the settlement, but he just hadn't made it. So maybe the buzzards would call the Sheep out in the daylight to find his bones. Or maybe the rustlers would take

away the remains and give him the kind of burial they'd
given Ruth's father. Be a damn shame for these fine boots
to be buried in the earth. Especially with his feet still in
them.

What the hell are you doing in a spot like this, *hombre?*
Why ain't you cozy in some *cantina,* cadging drinks off
the señoritas, huh? He wished there were some way of
knowing whether Ruth had made it to the cow camp.
Dammit, she *had* to. Well, *hombre,* you've just been wasting your life. Maybe you're wasting your death, too, huh?

It wasn't just the belly muscle aching now. He could
feel his gut curling into a downright unpleasant knot. The
waiting was worse than being chased. Let's get it the hell
over with, fellas.

Sure, that was what they wanted. They had him, so now
they were letting him sweat awhile before they finished it.
All right.

Stretched out on his side, he rammed the empties out of
the Remington. He mumbled a soft steady string of
curses in Spanish as he fingered fresh rounds out of the
belt loop and nudged them into the cylinder. For what
good it might do.

CHAPTER 15

Loco frowned as he caught the faint tremor. It was in the earth and in the air. It was growing into a sound. Hoof-beats. A bunch of animals, he thought. It couldn't be the ranchers on their way to attack the settlement, though. Even if Ruth hadn't been able to stop them, it was still too soon for them to be here.

A short cut through the morning stillness, stark as a gunshot. A wild, wordless yelp like the cry of a happy coyote.

Gunshots answered it. He heard the crack of rifles close by. Then more guns hollering from the distance.

Understanding, and grinning, he lifted his head to give a yell. *"Amigo!* DeVaca, damn you!"

The rumble of hoofs was getting louder. The riders were closing. The shots came faster. Furious yelps mingled with the clamor. And all of it was beautiful music.

Still grinning, he rose cautiously to his knees. He didn't draw fire. The men who'd chased him into this hole were suddenly busy with other problems. A dozen or more riders were bearing toward them, waving guns and hollering like all hell let loose. And the *caballero* silhouetted against the dawn sky in their lead was Ray deVaca.

The rustlers had been afoot, resting their tired horses. A couple of them got mounted up, trying to run. One headed toward the woods. But his animal was still close to exhaustion. And the attackers had fresh horses. Pushed hard, the rustler's mount staggered. He let it stop. It stood spraddle-legged and headhung. He turned in the saddle and tried snapping a couple of shots at the men behind

him. Then he tossed away the gun and wave his hands
in surrender.

The other man who had made it onto his horse turned
toward Loco. Maybe he didn't know or didn't much care
where he was going. Or maybe he just plain wanted to
finish the job he'd begun. Whatever it was, Bremen
lunged his mount toward the hollow where Loco'd hidden.

He had a revolver in his hand. But his horse was bounding with the jagged stride of weariness. He couldn't steady
the gun. He fired wildly. And he kept coming, as determined as a steam engine.

Loco's third shot flung him out of the saddle.

The horse didn't slow or swerve. It just kept coming in
a plunging, bobbing gallop. Loco jumped back out of its
path. He stumbled over his own dead mount and sprawled.
For a long moment, he just lay there, feeling like it wasn't
worth the trouble to get up. So damned tired himself.

But there seemed to be a small war going on around
him. Hoofs, shooting, shouting, the stink of burnt powder,
and above it all deVaca's shrill, happy war cry. Damn
you, you beautiful bastard, what took you so long? With
a sigh, he got himself up out of the dirt.

The three rustlers who had stayed afoot had tried for
cover, but there just wasn't enough of it. A few hummocks, some stubby brush, and grass that wasn't long
enough to hide a man. One of them screamed as lead hit
him. Another called quarter. The third lay motionless,
bad hurt or dead.

The attackers stopped their shooting and began to strug-
gle with their half-panicked mounts. Watching and grinning, Loco thought as how they were pretty rotten cavalry.
One came unseated, flopping into the grass and hollering
like a scared pig. Another clung to the saddle horn with
both hands as his horse took off for the tall timber of its
own accord. The rest managed to stay aboard and were
regaining control of their mounts. Rotten cavalry, but
lovely anyway.

"Hey, crazy man!" deVaca shouted, wheeling his horse

toward Loco. He came headlong at a gallop, bringing the animal to a rearing halt at Loco's side. "What you doing here, friend? How you like my soldiers, huh?"

"They're beautiful, you lousy chino. What the hell took you so long?"

"Next time you want me, write me a letter. Who we been fighting?" He gestured broadly at the field. "These ain't the ranchers we were expecting, huh?"

"No, they're the rustlers. Treat 'em nice and maybe they'll tell you all about it," Loco answered. He grabbed at the horse's mane, steadying himself. It felt like his knees were about to fold under him. The sense of urgency that had kept him going through the chase had deserted him, and with it, his strength. The Remington was getting too heavy to hold. He stuffed it into the holster.

"You all right?" Ray asked him.

"Yeah. Just tired. So damned tired." He clung to the mane of the horse, but his hand seemed to be slipping. He could feel a trembling in his knees. Right handsome horse, he thought dimly. He blinked, trying to clear the blur that washed across his vision. Hell, yes, it was that Three-Slash-C dun.

"You don't look so good. . . ." Ray was saying.

Loco opened his eyes, aware that it had been a long time since they'd snapped closed on him. He lay on a feather bed, with his head deep into a pillow. Glancing around, he found he was in the outbuilding behind Shepherd's cabin. He grumbled a soft curse.

DeVaca was hunkered across the room, messing around with something. Cleaning a pistol. He looked toward Loco. "You awake, friend?"

"Yeah," Loco grunted as he sat up. He blinked and squinted at the shaded window over his head. Bright sunlight outside. "How long I been asleep?"

"All day, all night, half of this morning. *Muy perezoso.* Very lazy." The word caught Ray's fancy. He singsonged it. "Lazy, crazy, crazy, lazy . . ."

"Go to hell."

"Been there already. You still sick, huh?"

"No," Loco answered. It was pretty near true. He felt plenty hungry, but that was about the worst of it. Rubbing at his face, he mumbled, "What the devil took you so long out there?"

Ray shrugged. "Didn't know you was waiting for me. My lookout seen all of you coming and we figured you was the ranchers gonna attack us, maybe something like that. We had a real fine ambush all ready for you. Oh, you should have come all the way, *amigo*. Such a beautiful ambush!"

"Well, when I didn't come spring your trap, why the hell didn't you get out to see what was wrong?" Loco grunted as he reached for a boot. He shoved his foot into it and tugged.

Ray gave him a look of injured innocence. "We did."

"You sure took your time about it."

"How do you say it, gringo? Better late than never. Hey, you got a letter."

Loco'd been pulling on the second boot. He paused, looking up sharply and scowling. "A *what?*"

With a grin, Ray held out an envelope. "From the lady of the ranch."

"Ruth? You seen her?"

"Sure. Yesterday, while you sleep so much, they come. Lots of *patrons*, all with their mouths full of sweet words. They love the Sheep, and now the Sheep love them, and everybody is friends, gonna all be happy forever. She was with them, very pretty, only with her arm in a bandage like she is hurt. She says to me, *no don't you wake him*. And she gets paper from Shepherd and writes you a letter." Ray waved the envelope. His grin looked a lot like a leer. "*Muy mujer*, huh?"

"Shut up," Loco growled, eying him with sharp anger. What the hell would a letter be about, he wondered. For sure, it was none of Ray's damned business.

Ray got slowly to his feet. He walked over and held the envelope toward Loco.

Taking it gingerly, Loco held it as if it were something hot. He frowned at it. Ray watched him with open amusement. At last, he handed it back, grumbling resentfully, "All right, what's it say?"

Ray tore the envelope and thumbed out the note. He gazed at it in silence, raised his eyebrows, and pursed his lips.

"I'll bash your damned head in," Loco said.

Shrugging, Ray began to read aloud. "Please come to the ranch. I wish to see you and thank you for your kindness. Most sincerely, Ruth Caisson."

"That's all?" Loco asked. It gave him an odd feeling. There should have been more. A lot more. But if there had been, he sure wouldn't have wanted Ray reading it.

Ray nodded. Leaning his head back, he laughed, then caught his breath and said, "Hey, we got to get going. Shepherd, he says, let him sleep. Only by sundown we got to get going. They don't 'bide thieves around here. Whiskey, either. Maybe we'll get to this town, this Gaff's Crossroads, by sundown if we leave soon. They got whiskey there, huh?"

"I may not be going with you," Loco mumbled as he jerked the boot the rest of the way on. He got to his feet and stretched, flexing his shoulder muscles.

"No?" Ray looked at him in surprise. "Where you gonna go? You can't stay here. The Sheep don't like you. Except maybe Shepherd's daughter. And Shepherd, he don't like you most of all."

"Where I'm going is none of your business. Have I got a horse?"

Ray hunkered to finish work on the gun. He answered, "Maybe I lend you one of mine. I got a good one I came here on, and a pretty coyote dun I sort of borrowed to ride while mine rested. Maybe I lend you my dun."

"*My* dun. Somewheres I got a bill of sale for that horse."

"Sure," Ray chuckled. "You never had a bill of sale for nothing in your life."

"I got one now," Loco grinned, thinking of Ruth. Of course she wouldn't write everything down in a letter. She'd say it to his face. That was why she wanted to see him.

He stretched again. The soreness in his belly muscle was about gone. He felt rested, real fine, ready for what came next. With a pleasant sense of anticipation, he added, "Yeah, and I got more'n that."

Ray laughed as if he didn't believe a word of it.

They rode together as far as the turnoff to the Three-Slash-C. As Loco halted the dun, Ray drew rein and looked at him seriously. "You sure you ain't coming?"

"Yeah."

"San Francisco. They say she's one hell of a town. Nice place."

"This is a nice place."

Ray shrugged. "*Sí*, only maybe you'll change your mind. You find Alfonso Garcia y Grenel, the tobacco man. He'll know where I am."

"*Sí*," Loco said. "*Adios, amigo.*"

"*Hasta luego*," Ray answered, gigging his horse. As he headed off, Loco watched him with a vague feeling of loss. Then he turned the dun toward the ranch house.

He saw Sundance by the corral, standing with reins looped over a rail. The saddle on the bay's back was a man's rig. He wondered if Ruth had decided she preferred riding astride. Grinning to himself, he hallooed the house.

She appeared from behind it, out of the kitchen. Her left arm was in a sling, but there was an apron over her sweeping skirt, and the sleeves of her calico shirt were rolled up. There was a smear of flour on her cheek, and wisps of hair straggled from the ribbon that held it. She looked very soft, very female.

Loco drew the dun up in front of her and stepped from the saddle.

She didn't meet his eyes. Glancing at his horse, she said thinly, "I see you got him back."

He nodded, startled by the strangeness of her voice. It wasn't exactly cold, but it sure wasn't warmly welcoming either. Not what he'd expected at all.

He began, "Bosslady . . ."

But she cut him short, rushing out the words. "I wanted to see you again, to thank you myself. I wanted to give you this—in appreciation—"

He frowned at the folded slip of paper she held toward him. This was all wrong. Every tone of her voice, every line of her face, all of it. All totally wrong.

"What is it?" he asked. He had that feeling of being out of place again, as if he were lost somewhere that he didn't belong.

"It's hardly enough. I could never really repay you for everything. But I thought—please understand." She thrust the paper at him anxiously.

"What is it?" he repeated dully, afraid that he did understand.

"Sundance. I know how much you think of him. I want you to have him."

"A bill of sale?"

She nodded.

Sighing, he mumbled, "Take it, *hombre,* it's all you're gonna get."

"Loco, please!" She looked as if he'd slapped her. *"Please* understand!"

"I reckon I do." His hand accepted the paper and stuffed it into his pocket. His fingers felt awkward, almost numb.

She was gazing up into his face with a look of hurting somewhere deep inside. A look of begging for him to ease the pain. There were small fires burning in those deep gray eyes. Her tongue flicked across her lips.

He caught her in his arms. Grabbed her mouth with his. He told her all of it in that kiss.

But she didn't answer. And that was an answer in itself.

She had been expecting the kiss, halfway hoping for it. She searched it and herself, and the response wasn't there. She accepted the kiss. She returned nothing.

Letting her go, he backstepped.

She wiped her mouth with her hand, unaware that she did it. Her eyes had a sadness in them. A trace of regret. Nothing more.

Loco swallowed hard. He asked, "That Martin stud?"

She shook her head. Her mouth formed a very small wistful smile. "No, not him. Not anyone I've met yet."

"Maybe . . ." he started. But he knew it was no use. When she'd responded to him before, up there on the slopes, she'd been weak and needing help. She had her strength back now. What she hunted now was more than just a man's presence and strength. What she hunted wasn't him.

And what he wanted here couldn't be taken. It had to be *given*, else it didn't happen at all. Shrugging, he worked up a grin. He hoped it didn't look as strained as it felt. "*Si*, bosslady. Thanks for the horse."

He wheeled away from her. Jerking loose the reins, he stepped up onto Sundance. The horse lifted its head, snorting. He could feel the eager vitality in it. Yeah, horse, let's get the hell away from here.

Take what you can, it's all you'll get, he told himself. There were two pieces of paper in his pocket. Two bills of sale. Leaning out of the saddle, he caught the dun's reins and said, "Thanks for *both* horses."

She didn't protest. She was still smiling in that small way when he looked toward her again. It was a gentle smile. There was a hint of dampness in her eyes and warmth tinged her voice. But not promise. She said, "Take care of yourself, Loco."

"I always do," he answered, gigging the bay.

He had almost reached the cutoff before he looked back. He could see her standing there. The smudge of flour would still be on her cheek, and there'd be a fire in that big black range, making ready to bake something tasty.

A warm cozy kitchen full of good eats. Pretty woman working at the stove. Bed upstairs covered with quilts. Acres of land. Horses and cattle.

It would have been pleasant, he thought. Real pleasant. For a while . . .

But the world was a big place, and a man could get mighty curious about the parts of it he hadn't seen yet. Yeah, a big country, and a lot of days yet to come. Bright fresh spring days, and sweaty miserable summer days, and brisk-dawned fall days, and ice-laden winter days, all just waiting up ahead.

California, huh? He'd heard tell that on the coast of California you could see the sun setting right down into an ocean. That sure must be a sight. A man couldn't go through his whole life without he ever saw a thing like that, could he?

He laid his heels to the bay's flanks, setting it into a lope. Damned fine horse. And another fine one trailing at his side. Bills of sale in his pocket for the both of them. Double eagle in his pocket, too. The sun warm on his back, and the scents of the day spicy with lush promise. A good day. And a good country for a man who was free to enjoy it. Lots more of both ahead.

Whistling cheerfully, he urged the bay into a gallop. Should be able to catch up with Ray before he reached Gaff's Crossroads. And this time he had coin in his pocket to pay that storekeeper for a round of drinks.

What the hell more could a man ask—and expect to get?

Lee Hoffman was born in Chicago, Illinois, and attended Armstrong Junior College in Savannah from 1949 to 1951. During her first college year she discovered science-fiction fandom and the vast network of correspondence and amateur publishing that it supported. She made many friends in this new world and even founded her own monthly magazine, *Quandry*, which attracted an enthusiastic audience. In addition to her interest in science-fiction, she continued to be an avid Western fan. Finally, in 1965, she completed a book-length Western of her own, *Gunfight at Laramie* (1966). Shortly after this first Western novel was accepted, Hoffman was commissioned by Ace to write a comic Western. It became her second book, *The Legend of Blackjack Sam* (1966), a novel all about "the Notorious Showdown at the O'Shea Corral." The years of writing for the amateur press and her own amusement were now paying off. *The Valdez Horses* (1967) is perhaps her masterpiece. Its emotional impact, aided by a surprise twist in the last line, make this novel difficult to forget. It received the Golden Spur Award from the Western Writers of America. In other novels such as *The Yarborough Brand* (1968) and *West of Cheyenne* (1969), no less than in *The Valdez Horses*, character and motivation are as important as details of the plot. It isn't that Hoffman skimped on action—there are fistfights, gun battles, and chases, but they serve the story rather than being the story's reason for existence. Hoffman refused to be predictable. In common with B. M. Bower before her and P. A. Bechko after, Hoffman tried her hand more than once at comic Westerns, notably in *Wiley's Move* (1973) and *The Truth About The Cannonball Kid* (1975). R. E. Briney in the second edition of the *Encyclopedia of Frontier and Western Fiction* concludes that Hoffman has always had "an enviable command of the writer's craft and the storyteller's art."